DESTINY OF DREAMS
Michael Bowler

A Paperback Original
First published 1990 by
Poolbeg Press Ltd.
Knocksedan House,
Swords, Co. Dublin, Ireland.

ISBN 1 85371 065 2

This book is published with the help of
The Arts Council/An Chomhairle Ealaíon, Ireland

Cover design by Pomphrey Associates,
Typeset by Print-Forme,
62 Santry Close, Dublin 9.
Printed by The Guernsey Press Ltd.,
Vale, Guernsey, Channel Islands.

DESTINY OF DREAMS
Michael Bowler

POOLBEG

To My Mother

In memoriam my father and Debbie
Amor Ipse Notitia Est

"The Boys from Barr na Sraide"
from *The Ballads of a Bogman* by Sigerson Clifford
published by Mercier Press, 4 Bridge Street, Cork, Ireland.

Whispering over the half-door of the mind,
For always I am Kerry

Sigerson Clifford

Prologue

For he comes the human child,
To the waters and the wild
With a faery, hand in hand,
From a world more full of weeping,
than he can understand.
                    "The Stolen Child"
                              by W B Yeats.

The mountain. Purple. The sky. Dark. The silence. Blue. Shadows between the skyline and the mountain. He turned back on the evening. Alone at eight.

Something in the stillness startled the boy and he tensed to run three fields down. Black fields which were green under his feet by day. His aunt's fields: his ranch during the summer holidays. Stopping suddenly, a meadow from Castlequin Road, he looked behind. The mountain loomed into the sky, looking dangerously down on him. Furze bushes seemed to move in secret. He shivered and hunched his shoulders for the dirt road leading through the dark buildings ahead. The haunted mansion, pointed to by some winter-sharpened trees. Lying menaced by mystery and ruined by age. Haunted by a poor widow's only son. Hanged because he had left a landlord's pig to die. The story ran through his head as he came round the gap into the yard, between the stables and the tall house. Eyes to the ground, afraid to look for fear of seeing someone. Halfway across the yard the frightened cawing of the crows made him start and run, raising the dormant wind to his face. He ran and ran, thinking his legs would turn to lead, like a nightmare and it was night. His grandmother's death night. The trees throwing

1

shaking shadows to the ground. The side of the house gaping crookedly at him. Now and then the birds would break from the branches and hang like night vultures in the uneasy air.

Finally he burst through the archway and produced another spurt from his tingling feet. Running easy now, further and further from the mad mansion, until it was just a silent memory. Gradually easing up he settled to a walk, letting his breath lighten the dark air. Thinking back he felt for a reason for his fright but could only see the parched face of his grandmother. He felt thirsty, his mouth dry with congealed fear. His grandmother again, in the small room at home, kept entering his mind. No door shut but another one opened, causing him to shake and walk faster. Faster and faster until he was racing again away from his grandmother and her home staring behind him. The wind swept like a cool hand across his forehead, clearing his head and cleaning his mind of dead images.

He never looked back again as he reached for the spikes of the great gate to vault over. In the main road he hurried into the beckoning lights of the town that stretched like a Y on the outline of the far hill. One fork probed into the hill, petering out by a lone farmhouse at the end of Letter. To take his mind from the black night he thought up a riddle. "Why does Cahirciveen look like a Y?" "Because it ends in Letter!" Hungry and chill over the bridge; the town lights making windows in the hollow river. Along the quay he came to Railway Street which the convent dominated. He felt a great relief on reaching Main Street. He walked past the little grocers where his grandmother used to buy a packet of Mikado biscuits. Every Friday without fail, when she called after collecting her pension. He thought of her then when she was alive, a tall figure in a black shawl. Walking slowly but upright past his window. Always slipping a sixpence into his hand when his mother wasn't looking. Passing the tiny shop made him feel sad. His stomach started to sink and a wave of loneliness welled up in him, rising as his stomach fell, to tickle his eyes. He felt the tears poised to paint his abject misery but he blinked them blindly away. It wasn't the sixpence that

2

bought his sense of loss but the image of their conspiracy as she turned her grey head, with the hairpins twinkling. Her glance: a half smile, half warning, brought him to her armchair as she whispered so many times. "Come over here now and open my fist." Years of Fridays he went to the chair by the fire, even in summer. Always a little shy of taking her money but knowing he'd have to open her long thin fingers, surprisingly strong in memory. Sometimes she would tease him as she locked his hand in hers and he pulled and pulled until she let go. Then he would fall and bounce on the lino, laughing up at her.

She was well then, before her fall. After her hip mended she visited the house with a stick. He played at 'Fair Days' with it but she had no laugh left. He soon stopped swinging the stick and sat between his mother and the open range as they talked. They spoke very low about the hospital and his grandmother's face looked so lonely that he interrupted without thinking, "You can stop here Nan, with us."

Her pale face softened as she looked across at him. "Oh no," "I'll have to go to St Anne's and you'll have to visit me." He said nothing. "You will, won't you?" She smiled at his silence.

His mother spoke with a firm look at him. "He has it there Nan, the front room is as good as any ward and they'll be nobody to bother you."

"Ah I don't know, it would be too much trouble entirely," his grandmother replied with a sway in her voice. His mother had put her foot down and his grandmother had no argument. Her face lit up slowly as they made arrangements for the following weekend, a week from Christmas.

The doctor called twice that week and the house was hushed. The Canon returned on Christmas Eve and stayed in the sick room a long time. He had left his tall black hat on the kitchen table and the boy's brother, Patches, two years his junior, kept trying it on. He had joined Patches and they were both laughing low when their mother caught them. "Will the two of you stoppit this instant. The Canon's hat is sacred," she added crossly.

"I've a sacred head so," Patches sang. He took the hat from

3

Patches saying, "We know, very sacred, look at the size of it."

She died that night, in silence but for the prayers of the house around her. In the morning the boy awoke early to find a Christmas stocking hanging on the end of the bed. Apple, orange, banana and a cap gun under a bag of toffees. His mother opened the door as he was loading the green reel of caps. He had already pulled the trigger at his brother's ear, but the first cap didn't explode. His mother's red-rimmed eyes stopped his second attempt and he twirled the trigger round his finger as she told them quietly: "Your Nan's gone to Heaven." The boy threw the gun in the wardrobe, still loaded. Dressed, he tiptoed downstairs one step by one. He didn't want to go into the deadroom but his father led him in. The room was still, with a different smell. The bed looked very white and her face soft against the brown habit. Hands cold in prayer, fingers entwined in her black rosary beads. Her life over and left holding hands only with herself. He was glad to get on his knees at his father's bidding, to look at the floor and rush through an 'Our Father, Hail Mary and a Glory.' Then he was told to go 'Over the Water' to tell his Aunt that his Nan was dead.

"Dead." He repeated the word. Felt it so black and endless like a winter's night. Thought it must be like being sick forever, only nobody got sick in Heaven. Dark. The road stretched under the broken ESB light, leading home. Coming round the bend he looked to his house. A light shone in the kitchen. It seemed dim in the distance. He wondered why his pal didn't call with his plaintive, "Will you be out?" He thought death was funny like that, keeping his pal away. Usually, hail, rain or snow wouldn't daunt him. Even a gale blowing against him couldn't stop him, arriving with his hair in the heavens. While he was going up to the garden gate a figure suddenly jumped out shouting, "You rascal, where did you take to today?" Heart jumping in his throat, the boy couldn't speak. "I'm here all day for you," his pal accused.

"Well you can be there all night for all I care," the boy finally spoke. "What did you frighten me for?"

"Ah! I only did it for a cod," his pal laughed.

4

"If you want a cod why don't you go fishing?" the boy spoke with recovered breath.

"Ah, drop dead! What's wrong with you at all?" his pal asked.

"My Nan dropped dead last night," the boy said quietly.

"——, did she, did she fall?" his pal rested a foot on the doorstep.

"Shut up, how can you fall in bed?" The boy was put out.

"You can too, you can fall asleep in bed" his pal laughed impishly. The boy didn't answer. "Is she in Heaven now?" he changed quickly.

"Course she is, she's a saint," the boy was indignant.

"What's her name so?" his pal pursued.

"Nan, Saint Nan," the boy said with faith.

"Isn't that the same as my Gran's name?" his pal was unimpressed and asked, "Are they all called that?" "They must have another name," he continued. "What about when they were young?"

"Must have so," the boy admitted. "I'll ask my mother," and as if remembering, he added "I'm hungry. Is it tea time yet?"

"Teatime!" his pal echoed. "I had mine hours ago."

"That was early," the boy said hopefully.

"It was dark," his pal disagreed. "Will you be out tomorrow?" he hesitated.

"Maybe. I'll be going to the funeral tomorrow," the boy said deliberately. "But I might be out Tuesday," adding "Will the ice be still on our skate rink?"

"If it freezes tomorrow it might," his pal hedged, taking his foot off the doorstep.

"I'm freezing now," the boy wrapped his arms round himself.

"Goodbye so," his pal started to move towards the gate but turned. "Are you listening to the match on the radio tomorrow?" he asked.

"It's off for my Nan," the boy raised his voice.

"Why? She can't hear it," his pal looking towards the gate, stopped again and muttered morosely, "I wouldn't like to be dead at all."

"It's wrong to have the radio on when my Nan is dead," the boy stated.

"She's not dead in my house; you can come over with me," his pal fumbled with the catch on the gate."

"I wouldn't be left anyway," the boy replied, and losing patience added, "I don't want to listen, anyway."

"It'll be great," his pal carried on.

"I know, but I wouldn't be left anyway," the boy answered emphasising "anyway."

"I'd better go home so, I'm here all day," his pal banged the gate and shouted as he went. "I'll call for you at eleven on Tuesday, be up!"

"See you and say a prayer for my Nan," the boy called out.

His pal turned surprised, "Why? She's in Heaven, what's she want a prayer for?" "I've got hundreds of prayers to say for living people," he exaggerated, but compelled by the boy's voice he relented. "Alright, just a 'Hail Mary' so, good luck."

"So long," the boy sighed deeply.

His pal went off, trying to whistle, and the boy lifted the knocker three times. His mother opened the door saying, "You're blue with the cold, hurry on into the fire."

He looked up from his blue knees to speak, "I'm starving hungry, Mam."

"What kept you?" she asked in the hallway.

"I met the scut," he replied.

"Oh, that manly bit, he never stopped calling all day." His mother started to fire questions at him. "Did you tell your Aunt Alice about Nan?"

"I did."

"Is she coming to town?"

"I don't know," he replied truthfully.

"Was Liam there?"

"No, but he came in as I was leaving."

"What did he say?"

"He said 'blow me'."

In the kitchen his other aunt was sitting with her legs open to the fire, a cup of tea in her hand. There was a strange woman sitting on his Nan's chair. "Is this the little boy?" she asked with a funny voice. He took an instant dislike to her, little indeed and he eight.

"Aren't you going to shake hands with your Aunt from England?" his other aunt coaxed him. He looked from one to the other before turning to his mother.

"Is my tea ready Mam?"

"Oh, the poor man's hungry, he hasn't the strength to shake hands with me." His English aunt was looking at him trying to win him with her shiny white teeth. Seated, he automatically turned towards the radio on the shelf by the glasscase. There was a blue apron draped across the fawn face. He wanted to heat his hands on the fire but it was surrounded by his aunts.

"Wash your hands, there's a good boy," his mother stood with the teapot poised over his mug.

He did as he was told, silently, and returned. Nobody was talking and he ate slowly so as not to be heard gulping. After a second cup of tea he started to read a comic but couldn't finish it because Patches came in from next door and began to play "cowboys" in the kitchen.

"Put him to bed, like a good boy and I don't want to hear a gug out of him till morning," his mother held the door open. "Get up them stairs this minute," she warned Patches who was skittish. He fell asleep while waiting for his brother to settle down, forgetting to ask his mother his Nan's young name.

Morning came, bright and hardy. The kitchen was full of people, all dressed up, sitting on the edges of chairs. After porridge and tea the boy's face was scrubbed by his mother. Two cars arrived and his mother took his hand in her black glove. The men had black bands around their arms and the women black everything. He had to sit on his mother's lap in one of the cars on the way to the Church. The aisles were filling and people turned their heads to look at him. Mass was very long and he grew tired of kneeling, so he sat up except when everybody stood.

The sun shone on the brown coffin, making it shiny and gold. Four men shouldered it; he thought one was an uncle but the other three were strangers. He imagined his grandmother in it but couldn't picture her face. He thought maybe her face had

7

gone to Heaven with her soul. His mother kept dropping his hand outside the Church because people were shaking both of hers. Nobody shook his hand and he wanted to tell them she was his Nan too. Crowds of mourners lined the two sides of the street as the hearse drove slowly to the graveyard. The boy was in the car that followed the hearse. Over the bridge the funeral went faster. He thought he saw his pal on the beach, skimming stones.

In the graveyard the priest stood at the top of the grave. The brown earth was hard with stones. The boy saw a snail wriggle through a clod and wanted to kill it. He knew they ate dead things. The coffin lay on a mound of earth, two ropes round it. The priest blessed himself in Latin and a decade of the Rosary was recited. It sounded like a murmur to the boy, the words blurred on the cold air. Drops of rain scurried round the huddle of people and the earth got browner. The priest's voice hurried to the sprinkling of holy water on the already wet coffin. The waters mingled without distinction. Finally, as the crying started the coffin was carefully lowered and the boy heard the earth suck at it as it reached the bottom. Shovels of earth falling punctuated the crying of his mother. His aunt from England had a white hanky covering her nose, her face red. The boy saw a girl-cousin looking at him and he didn't cry even though he wanted to. Holding tightly to his mother's hand he was led away as the grave was smoothed out with the flat of the shovel on the bare earth.

Home: they all had tea, first the grown-ups, then the boy, Patches and their cousins, who were laughing. They were from the country. The boy was bored with sitting quietly and asked if he could go over to his pal. He was down at the bridge and the boy ran all the way. His pal was still skimming stones, and the boy wondered was he at it when the funeral passed. He shouted his pal's name from the bridge, beckoning him. His pal waved back, unmoved. "It's not Tuesday today," his pal said indifferently when the boy climbed down to the strand.

"I know," the boy admitted.

"I saw the funeral passing," his pal said, matter of factly.

"I saw you," the boy said, adding "You should have stopped

skimming so."

"I did at the start but it was too long," his pal defended himself by estimating, "Was it a mile long?"

"'Spose so, maybe two," the boy gave up.

"What did you do when it rained?" his pal asked, stooping for a stone.

"Nothing, it was only a few drops, only wet my head." The boy brushed a damp lock from his right eye.

"Did you cry?" His pal skimmed a stone five times over the even water with his question.

"That was a good one," the boy didn't answer.

"Did you?" his pal persisted.

"No," the boy replied shortly.

"No?" his pal queried. "Cross your heart and hope to die."

"I didn't cry." The boy threw a light pebble that sank straight down.

"But you won't cross your heart?" his pal complained.

"I will if you won't believe me," and the boy said the words very fast.

His pal waited to see if he'd die and said, "I believe you," when the boy didn't fall.

"I passed the haunted house yesterday, in the dark, so how would I cry?" the boy had the last word.

"Did you see the mourning mother?" his pal stopped skimming.

"Not in the dark, silly," the boy said scornfully.

"I can see in the dark," his pal's eyes twinkled.

"You can, so?" the boy snorted.

"I can," his pal paused. "I can see a light in the dark,"

"Ah, you're mad," the boy flung a stone with one skim."

"Will we go over to see if she is out or not?" his pal suggested.

"No." "It's too bright for her to be out," the boy wasn't interested.

"Funky!" his pal accused.

"Of what? That old house?"

The boy coloured under his collar. "Anyway I don't believe it's even haunted," he added.

"Well, come over so," his pal challenged.

The boy threw one last stone saying, "Alright."

They moved as one, climbing the bank to the road. The day was beginning to draw in as they made their way to the house. The boy had one hand in the new trousers, the other swinging a sallyrod that he broke from the ditch. His pal walked close to him, two hands deep in his torn pockets. The wind was rising unnoticed in the shelter of the high ditches. The mountain above the house darkened slowly as a black cloud moved west. Passing the graveyard they blessed themselves silently. The boy shivered thinking of his grandmother in the cold earth. Arriving at the gate, they hauled themselves over the spikes without speaking. Halfway up to the house his pal broke the silence.

"It's getting dark."

"It's only a cloud," the boy answered detecting a reluctant note in his pal's voice.

"Nobody really lives here, do they?" his pal was whispering.

"No, except the woman," the boy paused, remembering.

"And her boy too."

"What about her boy?" his pal questioned.

"He's dead," the boy said flatly.

"Was he old?" his pal took one hand from his pocket.

"Eight, I think, our age," the boy answered, patiently.

"God!" "How did he die?" his pal continued.

"He was hung up," the boy indicated the sallyrod in the air.

Their shoulders touched as they moved closer. Their steps slowed as the ruin reared up before them. The arch of the courtyard opened like a dark mouth as they entered. His pal looked behind him as the trees trembled in a sharp gust. "Ah, it's only the wind," the boy's voice shot from the hollow walls and echoed back.

"What?" his pal shouted, and the answer bounced back from the walls. His pal clutched his arm. "Somebody spoke. Did you hear that?"

"What?" the boy shouted back feeling his arm.

"Somebody spoke," his pal repeated.

"You did," the boy told him.

10

"I know, but somebody answered me," his pal's voice faltered.

"That was an echo, you gom," the boy released his arm.

"Oh, it gave me a start," his pal said in a small voice.

They made their way deeper into the yard, glancing to the aged walls. Dark holes gaped back at them. They turned the tall tree standing in the middle of the courtyard. Alone. Bare branches limp, like dead fingers pointing to the earth. "That's the tree he was hung up on," the boy touched the base with the sallyrod. In silence they stood under the outlined tree. "It's a bit spooky an' all," the boy admitted.

"Look at that hole, is it a tunnel do you know?" his pal pointed. A large hole starting at the stump, slanted down.

"Might be, maybe the woman haunts from there," the boy answered, moving towards it. Again, together, they walked, a hand in one pocket, a sally in the boy's other hand and his pal's freely swinging. That's why the boy's mother called his pal "a manly bit."

The cloud drifted away west and the winter light lived again. The two boys stood at the edge of the hole, peering hard. The boy pitched a stone from the heap of earth round the hole and dropped it down. Silence. "Straight down," the boy said abating his breath.

"Australia's down there isn't it?" his pal asked, amazed.

"Far below that stone I'd say, but it's deep enough anyway." The boy toed some earth into the hole.

"She's hardly there, is she?" his pal asked hopefully. The boy was thinking of his grandmother again and didn't answer. "Come over here now and open my fist," a hand reached out from the far side of the hole, slender and pale. The boy hesitated before calling, "Nan, is that you Nan?"

"Who else would it be child? I've sixpence in my fist, you'll have to open it first." The hand clenched into a fist and the boy reached for it and caught a tiny fist for a moment. Then he felt himself falling, like sleep, falling into a deep darkness.

His pal screamed before hauling himself from the ledge he'd just noticed and climbed onto. His hand, a fist locked to his screaming mouth. Silence, like the stone. The pal went cold all

11

over, looking into the endless darkness. The tree shook stiffly in a rising wind but he didn't feel the cold outside. Tears gathered like torrents and streamed down his face. Blindly he turned and ran; the memory of the other boy's secret rushing through his mind. Across the courtyard, crying the boy's name over and over into the wind.

The mountain. Purple. The sky. Dark. The silence. Blue. Shadows between the skyline and the mountain. He turned back on the evening. Alone at eight ....

Chapter 1

"Across the street, leaves blow,
Across the trees, birds cry—
Across the mountains, far away,
My home must be."

Hermann Hesse

Seven seasons turned in time ....

Soon came the world of ten. To run through the night forest
without cracking a twig. To bend under a low branch without
crawling. To sit around the camp fire in a clearing with ...
Truth on our lips, strength in our limbs and purity in our hearts.
But where in Cahirciveen were the forests. How to run with
Truth when there was only the black strap to run from. Terror
of innocents: hung between the myth and the madness. Warned
to go to Christ and warned to stay from Coffey the tinker.

But I would sneak away to meet Johnny because he was my
best pal now and he could make a bicycle from bits and bolts
found in the dump. I spent my time looking over my shoulder
in case the Brother would see me with him. Somedays when I
reached the dump I forgot and rooted with Johnny who spotted
things I thought were useless. Johnny would lay each rusty
item in a line. Treasure. He never called the collection anything
but treasure. And me ... he'd call me by my first name which
none of the other boys did. Sometimes I'd forget and call him
Coff. But when I called him Johnny he looked at me as if I
called him God. Great. And he was great. He'd give me his last
gobstopper, sometimes out of his mouth. His pet name for me
was "nickle treasure" because I was small and he couldn't

13

pronounce "little."

Whenever I thought of him I remembered the poem the teacher used to make him recite:

The Snare

"I hear a sudden cry of pain,
There is a rabbit in a snare,
Now I hear that cry again,
But I cannot tell from where.

But I cannot tell from where,
He is calling out with pain,
Nickle one, oh, nickle one,
I am searching everywhere."

And I felt the pain on his face as he slouched to his feet; the eyes of the class laughing cold over his face, the colour of his hair. I'd clench my hands and will him to say little LITTLE and I knew the flushed fear that made him falter and mutter "nickle." He would have loved that poem if he hadn't been taught to hate it.

He used to set snares before he learned it and he told me he cried the first evening he trapped a rabbit. He learned the pain for the second time that day and set it free. And I imagined a little red-headed boy alone in a summer field, the blue rain streaking his freckles. his supper limping into a black burrow, the snare trapped in his clenched hands. I wanted to invite him for tea but knew I had to wait until I grew up and had a home of my own. I imagined "little rabbits in a field at evening lit by a slanting sun." Patrick Pearse wrote that line and I saw it when the sun set in Johnny's eyes. The poet Pearse died for that image of pastoral peace, died that "the bare-footed children playing in the streets of a little town in Connaught would have shoes." Died for Johnny, in vain because he couldn't see the future. The future where a small town teacher would murder the spirit of a child. A big country footballer who taught like he played football—by fear and favour. The murder machine.

Johnny lived in a house above the town, almost in the hill. The hill was called Beenatee. it meant behind the houses. His father was a traveller. His mother had lumbago. The caravan was a cold home in the winter wind. Johnny's father came home every Christmas. He was arrested the day of the Wren the year Johnny was kept back in fourth class. He was asleep in the trap; the piebald pony trotting home the short cut, a dirt road farmers used for driving cattle to the fair. It was parallel to the main road and called the Rocky Road. He was stopped by the squad car and the Guards reined in the pony who was cantering away in the middle of the road. A Guard shook the sleeping bundle and asked where was his light. "Don't ax me, ax the driver" was the only answer he got and Johnny's father was arrested. He called the Guard a stump of a fool for arresting the wrong criminal. The judge let him off with a warning. He became know as Axme after that.

It was the spring of that new year and Johnny and I planned to join the caravans. The air had softened. The smell of furze burning had me longing for a home under the stars. The nights were whitened by the young moon. One evening after school Johnny and I went up the Rocky Road to Primrose Wood. The flow of the winter rains was still strong in the ditches. Johnny had a box of matches and was going to light a fire. In a clearing we gathered twigs. Johnny broke a lath that was loose from the thorny wire that fenced the fields above the road. While Johnny kindled the fire I went looking for two slabs to sit on. In the light of the slow flames Johnny told me about the travelling life. Looking into the fire, his eyes lit by light and longing. Told me about the fireside stories, the banjo music and the songs. Summer nights between tall grass and sky. The dawns of picking mushrooms when the dew and the sun drenched the fields. Rounding up the piebalds and freeing the tethered goats. Talked of the excitment of fair days when Jacko, his uncle, challenged the farmers to a duel of strength. Nobody could beat him at lifting weights and he always gave Johnny a half-crown.

The fire went out when Johnny stopped speaking. An early moon half showed over the top of the hill. Johnny kicked the embers black with the sole of his torn shoe. he turned to me.

"Will you be with me now that I've told you the story?"

And I answered "I'll always be with you Johnny. We'll be blood brothers?"

Johnny heard the question in my voice and ruffled the back of my head, saying "Aren't you foxy enough for it."

We parted at the top of Fair Field, Johnny going home by the Old Road and I turning down to Main Street. Home, with the excitement of the secret on my cheeks. My sister, Breda opened the door "Mam'll kill you, where did you go to?"

"As far as turn back."

She was twelve and practising to be a mother.

I didn't talk to her except in insults. The half-past six news was on, the radio crackling. My mother was pouring out my father's tea. Sausages were sizzling in the pan on the range.

My mother said "came the day you promised" without pausing with the teapot. She talked in riddles sometimes.

"He's never broken his word yet," my father teased, sticking his cap on my head as I passed inside his chair.

"You can't break a word don't you know."

I plonked the cap back on his head, the peak to the back.

Breda said "huh, of course you can."

"Listen to Miss Samson there. I suppose you hit with a bigger word, like a hammer," I mimicked a girl.

"Not a hammer smartie, a hyphen."

I didn't know what a hyphen was so I stirred my tea noisily.

"Hurry up or you'll be late for the rosary." My mother put the plate of two suasages and the soft egg before me. One sausage had burst and I forked it, holding it before my eyes.

"I wonder did her holiness cook this? No wonder it burst its sides, laughing at you," and I held it before Breda's face. She put her nose in the air.

"You heard what your mother said," my father spoke. I ate fast and long, finishing a square of brown bread. My father was eating silently, listening to the news.

"Suez is bad," he said to my mother when it was over. They often talked of people, relations and friends I didn't know. I didn't know Sue anyway. After tea I did a few sums on the table, still wet after the wipe of my mother's damp cloth. I wasn't with my younger brother, Patches, so I pretended he wasn't there, sitting at the other end of the table. He found the big marble, my bomber, that got lost, and said it was his own. He lied a lot. Now I was waiting for him to flourish the other one, a taw. My older sister was working in the convent. She was fourteen and got twenty-five shillings a week. I didn't see much of it. She wore nylons. They were always running. Fast. She was my favourite. My choice wasn't up to much.

It was twenty five past seven when I finished my sums. My mother and Breda had already gone. My father was reading the Irish press under the bulb in the centre of the kitchen. On the way out I dipped my fingers in the holy water font at the side of the door. It helped to keep me away from harm. It didn't, not always, but I didn't take chances. I shivered when I pulled the front door shut. The moon had cleared the hill and I raced it as far as the Church.

The first decade was on. They were saying the joyful mysteries with long mournful voices and faces. I crept up the side aisle looking out for Johnny's red head. He wasn't there; the primary class Brother was. His red, bald head, shone in the lights. He was sitting under the cross. Johnny said he was only sucking up to the boss. The Canon was saying the Rosary so I settled down. He was as slow as a wet week. I looked up at benediction to see who was serving. Paul Lucey and Moocher Main. I heard the big boys call Lucey "Pauline" because he walked like a girl and couldn't play football. Moocher got his nickname for mooching from school. The Brother called it mitching. He was from Cork. He sent the Guards out after Moocher once. I saw the Sergeant pushing him by the collar past the window. That was the last time he did it. I inhaled the smell of incense as I genuflected to leave the Rosary.

Nightclouds had wiped the moon from the sky. I didn't linger outside the Church gates as the other boys did, huddled in secret. Camo's doorway straight across from the Church was full of secondary school boys. Some of them writing into copybooks stuck up against the second door. I knew they were cogging the maths. The maths teacher was hard, I heard. I

17

wasn't looking forward to going upstairs. The Inter classroom was over ours and the commotion was woeful. Sometimes the sting of the cane echoed in my mind and I shivered with dread. I stopped thinking of school, knowing if I put it from my mind I wouldn't feel cold. I wondered why school should make my mind go cold. My shoulders shook again because the night came down and I felt alone. I stopped at Breen's the butcher, to see what film was on Saturday night. It was a cowboy and the cold melted from my mind.

My father was asleep under the bulb, the paper spread across his knees. He woke, snorting through his nose.

"Where's your mother?" he asked, eyes pinched with sleep.

"Coming," I answered, because I wasn't God.

"Did you leave Carlow at the creamery Dad?" I asked, still standing.

"No, he's abroad in bed."

"I must see him." I rushed to the back door. Taking the flashlamp from my father's bike I unlocked the back door. Opening the turf shed door I heard him crying in his sleep. I didn't understand how dogs could think because they didn't have souls. Carlow must have been dreaming of herding cows. He was a sheepdog but there were no sheep at the creamery. Maybe that was his dream. "Carlow," I whispered, but he was awake when I shone the light on him. He wagged his tail, his eyes softened and he put up his head to my free hand. I put down the lamp and knelt on the turf-dust covering the floor. He licked my face and I rubbed his forehead. I heard my mother call so I said "go to bed Carlow" in a firm voice. It wasn't hard enough and he kept pressing his face into my hand. "Bed," I said coldly and his tail dropped. I picked up the lamp and gave him one rub along the white patch that divided his forehead.

"Haven't you any notion of going to bed?" my mother spoke from the scullery.

"He's plenty of notions after the blonde across the way," Patches piped up. He was by our father's chair so I couldn't do anything but blush and tell him "flip off."

"At least I haven't notions after other people's property," I took my chance "She isn't other people's property, she's

God's," Breda said in her matter-of-fact voice.

"Marbles," I replied, "are … "

"Blasphemy," she cut in with her shocked voice. She had a different voice for every word.

"Ah, Breda, he's talking about mebs, not his girlfriend," Patches laughed at her. Breda struck her head into the mystery of Fatima, a puzzled look giving way to a blank stare on her face.

"Oh," was all she said and patches tried to wink at me but only managed to close both eyes at once. I tried to wipe the bubbling smile from my lips but burst out laughing.

"Right, off to blanket street the two of you, right after your cocoa," my mother silenced us.

Patches said, "Right, right!"

I sat with Patches at the table in the alcove. My mother put a dessert bowl in front of me and spooned goody from the small warmer.

"Can I have more sugar?" Patches urged, imitating Breda's drawn out voice. My mother raised her voice to the ceiling saying "give me patience." The boiled white bread and milk was steaming and I blew on it to cool.

My father was silent, his head nodding on his chest. My mother brought him a big cup of cocoa. He took it and gave Patches a sup. Patches supped everything, even Carlow's milk, from a plate. I felt warm after eating and my eyes started to droop.

"Now off to bed small things," my mother stood by the kitchen door, her hand on the handle. Breda didn't stir. She thought it was beneath her to be called small. Patches wanted a hobby horse and I swooped down, forgetting I wasn't supposed to be with him. That was the trouble, when I fell out with him he let on I was the best pal in the world.

"Nighty, night," we both called out, and our father said "God bless".

"I'll be up in ten minutes and I want you both asleep with the light out," my mother warned as we went laughing upstairs.

I thought she didn't want much, for us to be asleep in ten minutes with Patches kicking the ribs out of me.

Upstairs I knelt side by side with Patches, saying my night prayers.

"As I lay down to sleep,
To God I give my soul to keep,
If I die before I wake,
To God I give my soul to take."

I said them quickly, mother's ten minutes in my mind. Patches finished first, as fast as I was. He didn't know many prayers. I took off my shoes before my clothes. My cross-over jumper caught on my head and I heard a rip when I pulled it clear. Patches was in bed when I could see again, his eyes wide open and holding two marbles out to me.

Chapter Two

Morning ....

My mother's voice calling as she always did "quarter to, out with ye." Friday. The day of the *Kerryman* paper. Looking to see was the school football team in it. My mother read the news from the county first. Under a town heading: parochial pride paraded. Someone won money in the silver circle. An exile won a medal in London. A boy got seven honours in the Leaving. Leaving … I thought of my plan as I dressed. I drew the curtain; the highest of the hills, Knocknadobar, faced the window and it seemed for an instant that I was drawing the curtain over the cross of Christ on the summit. Dawn delayed about the Hill of the Wells. Turning into the room I shook Patches as I made to go down to breakfast.

"What day is it?" he mumbled under the quilt.

"Fish day," I called over my shoulder.

He made me laugh sometimes. He could never remember the days, even got up once to go to school on a Sunday. My mother getting ready for Mass had to run after him as he strolled along trailing his bag. In a way I felt I'd miss him most of all.

"Here, get this inside you before it gets cold," my mother greeted me.

"Is Pat up yet?"

"He's getting," I answered sitting at the edge of the table and warming my hands on the steam rising from the bowl of gruel.

My mother was trying to get the nine o'clock news on Radio Eireann. The radio was up on a stand screwed to the wall. My father made it. People said he'd gifted hands. I didn't think much of the present when I got a clip across the poll.

The morning hung still above the housetops. I could see out

21

the front window as I supped my tea. I felt sleepy, like the morning, waiting to open. Patches rushed down the stairs shouting. "Mammy, it's Saturday today?"

"No it's not, child of grace. Will you put on your school trousers." He had put on his Saturday jeans and the light on his face died slowly. He turned, muttering "bleddy school," under his breath.

My mother said "will you wait for him," as the news ended. Quarter past nine. I had another cup of tea while Patches gulped his gruel. He was on his feet first. "Come on, we'll be late." He was all action, grabbing his schoolbag from the sofa. He had a green canvas bag our elder sister used to have. She hadn't made much use of it.

I walked quickly, passing the limping postman on the way. The air cleared my head and I could even listen to Patches rambling on. He was all set to climb Beenatee to see the Bull, Cow and Calf. Three rocks close together fusing like animals from afar. If I knew Patches he'd try to bring them home with him too. The Main Street was quiet except for the boys from the Island cycling swiftly past the Church. The Valentia ferry must have been delayed. Beyond the Island lay the Skelligs and beyond the Skelligs the nearest land was America.

The playground was empty and white looking. At eleven it would fill up with sound and colour. I looked in the window of the primary class. The black figure with the high red head was at the blackboard. I conveyed Patches to the first door before running back to the middle room. My heart skipped a beat when I looked in the dim window. The class was standing for morning prayers. I waited with my hand on the wooden knob, until the subdued murmuring petered out.

"Amen, to you young sir," the teacher unclasped his praying hands and greeted me. I coloured at the laughter that shook the classroom. Closing the door I went past him and ducked as he made to cuff my ear. The blonde wave was poised above his forehead, swept over his eyes. He was more mad at that than at me, and Johnny winked as I passed the first seat over by the front window. I sat behind him, next to the dentist's son. Just as the class was settling down the Primary Head came in and faced the class after a word with Mister Lyne.

"Hands up all you boys who attended the Rosary last evening." The silent hands pointed to the ceiling. The country boys were excused and Johnny was left sitting alone.

"Come here," the Brother beckoned, his finger close to his long red nose.

Johnny got up slowly, the hole in his jumper showing a circle of dark red shirt on the small of his back. With his shoulder slumped and his head bowed he looked like a wounded animal.

"What excuse have you this time Coffey?"

"The pony strayed, sir," Johnny's answer came, muffled in his chest.

"The pony strayed, sir" the Brother imitated him.

I set my lips when the blow came. Johnny's head jerked back, his eyes wild with dread.

"Look at me when I speak to you boy," the Brother's face turned another shade of red. His mouth twisted, spit whitening the corners.

"Same old excuse. Can't you tie the silly animal up?" the Brother's voice was pitched. I looked at the teacher. He was patting his wave and looking at his nails. Johnny stood looking sullenly at the silent figure before him. The Brother stared at him a long, long time. The clock struck the quarter hour. "May as well be talking to the wall as talking to you," he finally said and, turning to the teacher, "give him six slaps of the cane."

He turned and flounced out of the room, his black skirt swishing as he went. His name was Brother McGraw but we all called him Baldy McGraw.

The teacher took out the cane from the drawer in his desk and set the tips of Johnny's fingers straight. The stinging sound broke the morning air. Johnny rubbed his hands, holding his face from crumbling. I saw the two tears form at the outer corners of his eyes as he turned into his seat.

Mister Lyne corrected the sums we had for homework. I had one division wrong and got a slap of the black strap. It had pennies in it to make it hard. Some of the boys said they were half-crowns. My father said the Brothers had money to burn. Our hands.

23

During the break at eleven Johnny and I went up to the top corner of the playground. There was a kind of open chimney where the secondary boys smoked.

"He's done it now," Johnny said blowing on his hand. "We take to the road tomorrow, are 'ou coming?"

I saw Patches playing at the bottom of the playground and hesitated.

"Who're you looking for?" Johnny said following my eyes through the milling boys. Most of them were having hunts.

"Patches, my brother," I said, pointing him out.

"He's not as fairly as you," Johnny alluded to Patches' hair. "I see no patch on him anyway," he continued. "What gave him that name?"

I told him about the time when Patches was four. My mother used to ask him who was the best boy in the world. He couldn't say "Pats is" properly and so said "Patches" instead. I was always explaining it. I thought it was about time he learned about it himself. He must be the only one in town who didn't know.

The two Brothers were walking back and forth across the playground with Mister Lyne between them. Brother Long was Patches's teacher. He was very tall with rimless glasses perched on his nose. He was easy and told great stories about ghosts. They were never very holy either. Even Johnny liked him. He'd sent him up to the Secondary Superior for a round square and a glass hammer on April Fool's day when we were in second class.

The bell went and I finally said "I told you yesterday I'd go, Johnny. Only one thing, can I take Carlow?"

Johnny shouldered me gently "You can take the thirty-two counties if you want," he smiled and his face lit up with delight.

I smiled too and shouldered him back. Carlow was the name of a county too.

We had Irish when we went back. The country boys were best. They had the thick accent to go with it. Johnny couldn't make head nor harp of it. It was a musical language. He hadn't a note in his head.

At twelve there was religious instruction. Johnny had no

catechism so the teacher told me to sit with him. He sat on his own the rest of the time. The dentist's son would never be asked to share his desk. I had the same feeling as when I wanted the Indians to win in a western. Johnny was the outsider.

We were learning the commandments. I knew eight of them. I didn't know what the sixth one meant. Johnny said the eighth one meant a girl had a baby without being married ... "Bear false witness." I knew that was wrong because only married people got babies, from heaven. I was found floating in a basket down Carhan river myself. I wondered how it was I didn't capsize.

I waited outside the green gate for Patches at half-twelve. Johnny went out the Rocky Road to Carhan Wood. It was across from the river. He intended to gather nuts. Sometimes I thought he was nuts. I raced Patches to the Cross, giving him odds to the Post Office. He ran straight down the street while I took the footpath. I ran down by the dance hall and up by the side of the Church. That gave him an extra lead but I caught him at the Anchor Bar. We walked the rest of the way home, Patches linking my arm. My father was eating whiting. He said "fighting" for whiting. That's how people spoke in the country. I had fried eggs and pandy. I melted some more butter until the potatoes were dripping with yellow. My parents were talking about my elder sister. She wanted to go to an all night dance out the country. My mother was forbidding her but my father said "she may as well have her fling while she's young." Besides hadn't they got perfect permission from the Canon himself, so long as it wasn't on Saturday night. They agreed to allow her by the end of dinner.

I went up to my room after eating to sort my things for the journey. I took the fair day stick my father gave me out from under the mattress. Skimps of brown paint had peeled from the roundy knob. My toy soldiers, my marbles, my ... but that's all I owned. The cap gun I'd long since given to Patches.

I asked my father for fourpence for the *Our Boys*. It had good riddles and scary stories. I liked the tales about "Kitty the Hare" best because Patches was frightened to silence when I read them to him in bed. It made me feel snug and safe under the blankets. My father said "haven't you Our Boys enough in your books," but my mother coaxed the money out of him.

We had English after dinner, my favourite subject. At three o'clock the teacher told us all to close our books. "The Snare." He asked the class for recitation, starting at the back row. I had it off by heart when the time for my turn came. Johnny was after me and the teacher who'd been walking across the room, smiling to himself now and then, stopped in front of him. Johnny stared at the desk as he always did when questioned and started slowly. He paused before "little one" and in that comma, I whispered "little." Johnny repeated it "little one." The teacher echoed "el little. How small is that?" Johnny stumbled and I bit my lip. "I mean 'nickle one'," Johnny fell into the trap.

The teacher said "That's more like it for you" and the class laughed meanly.

"Now Coffey, tell me who prompted you?"

Johnny hung his head and I blurted out "I did sir."

"Ah men," he played to the gallery, not letting me forget the morning "and pray tell us why?"

"He's my pal," I said simply.

"He's *your* pal," he repeated, leaning heavily on "your."

That's all he said. He clouted me then, his long pale hand reaching past Johnny's ducking head. I felt my nose sting and fill until the blood ran into my mouth. Water came to my eyes and I saw Johnny swing round, his face whitening. I cupped my mouth and my hand ran red. In the time I stood dazed, my tears weakening the blood in my hand, Johnny moved. Grabbing my hand he pulled me to the aisle, at the same time lashing out at the teacher's legs with the side of his ruler. The footballer in him made him guard his legs and I was running by him without the help of Johnny's hand. Johnny turned the knob and then faced the class.

"The tinker's curse on you. God blast it, may your blood run black, you 'nickle' excuse for a man. You'd do right to draw blood. You'll never make little of me again," Johnny shouted at the stunned teacher, jumbling all his words together. The door slammed and I saw the teacher through the window, walking with his blonde head downcast, to his desk.

26

"Do you know what you just said?" I forgot my hurt.

"I know, 'twasn't strong enough but I couldn't think of worse," Johnny shook his head in regret.

"Not that, you said 'little', the right way," I told him patiently.

"Did I say that?" Johnny looked sideways at me.

"No you never said 'that', you said 'little'," I told him again.

"Ah, sugar off!" Johnny said sourly.

We walked together into the empty playground.

"Here," Johnny clutched my arm, "we'll go'ut the back door for fear Baldy'll see us."

Over by the bicycle shed a green door led out to the Fair Field. At the wall by the door a water tap hung, dripping. I got out my hanky and Johnny took it and soaked the corner under the tap. Taking my jaw he held my face up and wiped the dry blood from my nose.

"It's not as bad as it looks. You'll be better by the day you get married," he said handing me back the stained hanky.

"Where are we going?" I asked looking out the door.

The street, without people, made me feel Johnny and I were alone in the world. It was a strange feeling not knowing where to go, like living in a doorway.

"Home," Johnny said over my shoulder.

"Home," I repeated it like a new word, just learned.

"I can't go without my schoolbag, I'll be killed," I exaggerated.

"Your brother will be let out in a minute. Send him to get it, if you're afraid," Johnny added.

He didn't attach any importance to schoolbags.

Patches' class came charging into the playground before I could answer back. I pressed Johnny's arm to stay and ran over to the first door. I had to wait awhile before Patches came through, lost in earnest conversation with a thin boy with rimless glasses. They were arguing about the colour of the moon. Patches' face was red, a sure sign he was losing, and I heard him say "it's bleddy black," before he saw me.

"Pat," I called him by his proper name so he'd know I was serious. "I left my schoolbag behind. Will you get it for me?"

He opened his mouth in a question but the set of my face changed his mind. Without a word he went round the gable while I waved victory to Johnny. Patches never came back. Instead the bare red head of Brother McGraw showed round the gable. I wanted to run only my feet were made to the concrete. I looked to Johnny but he'd scooted. I stood my ground. The black figure settled before me.

"What's the meaning of this? Why did you leave the classroom before the bell?" He looked down to me over his pointed red nose.

"No why," I answered shortly, glancing once at his face.

He said nothing for a moment and I was raising my head again when his open palm slapped across my ear. My head seemed to explode with pain, my eyes stung with tears. I took one step back, my mind blazing. Words, hard words I didn't know I had lay hot and heavy on my tongue. I almost formed one, instead I bit my lip, looked coldly at him and turned my back.

"Where do you think you're going boy?" he called after me. I walked slowly to the green door. I expected him to grab me by the shoulder. I never looked behind and only put my hand to my ear when the door was safely shut. I looked up the Fair Field for Johnny. The hill alone looked down on the empty green. Early night darkening the outline where Beenatee met the sky. I felt empty; the image of the hill at night looking down over me made me feel trapped, locked in a black field. I stood, timeless, watching—felt the Fair Field to be the Garden of Gethsemane. Betrayed by the Brother with the collar of Christ. I felt the hard blood still blocking my nose. Felt ... my open eyes water ... and the rains inside me streamed down my face. Deep and silent rains washing the night from my soul. I stood watching, and watched alone.

Chapter Three

Someone was brushing the tears from my face. Someone with a gentle hand that smelled of ink. Another hand went round my shoulders. I blinked my eyes and Johnny's face, pale with faded freckles, was suddenly serious before me.

"Are you alright nickle treasure?" he said, giving my shoulder a shake.

"I thought you'd gone." My voice was weak.

"Ah, no boy," Johnny shook his head, "I only scooted so as Baldy would give you a fair shake."

"He shook me right enough," I said, "but there was nothing fair about it."

"Do'mind," Johnny said, "here's your bag at least."

I'd forgotten about Patches and my bag.

"I went round the front gate and took it from your brother," Johnny explained. "He's a hard man, he called me a piebald jennet and took me with a kick in the shins."

I laughed, I could just imagine Patches.

Johnny was fingering his shins. "He's a bit of a piebald himself the way he kicks."

I looked to the Fair Field again but the image of the suffering garden was swept away. I uttered more to myself than to Johnny, "I thought the Fair Field was the Garden of Gethsemane.

"Gethsemane," Johnny echoed, "is far from the Fair Field, in the Holy Land, and this land is only a holy show," he added, nodding his head to the school. I laughed at Johnny's joke but it was a hollow sound because what I felt was true.

"Come on, we better buzz off home," I said, hoisting my bag onto my shoulder. My fingers were cold. The night was setting in.

I strolled home silently, listening to Johnny's planning for the morrow. The light came on the ESB poles as we passed the Church. I blessed myself carefully on passing the tower door. Johnny made a quick rigmarole with one hand.

The convent school was let out the same time as us. I lengthened my legs as we came to the top of Railway Street.

"Jeepers, what's the express?" Johnny muttered half running to keep up with me.

"I'm," I paused, "I'm hungry."

Johnny said, "Hah, hungry," and under his breath something about "townies." I glanced down Railway Street at the noisy group of girls, trying to pick one fair head out. Johnny didn't even bother looking; he thought girls were a mistake. He made enough without their help. I spotted her halfway down, holding her young sister's hand. When I crossed beyond Railway Street I slowed down and Johnny was left pelting along on his own. He turned back at the Munster and Leinster bank. His flaming hair looked subdued in the gathering of night. His face trapped in a sad profile made me wish he was my brother. We could go all the way home together.

Together we fell into step without speaking. We came to Breen's the butcher's and stopped to look at the film poster; Johnny read the titles out loud. There was a different picture Tuesday and Thursday, Saturday and Sunday showed the same.

"We'll miss Geronimo tomorrow night," Johnny said at the end. I was glancing back while Johnny was reading. She was at the bank and the lights from the ESB poles set glints off in her hair. As she approached I pretended to read the red print on the poster. Presently she passed by, her curved lips tightened when she saw me with Johnny. Her fishnet white stockings stood out against the pale concrete. I nudged Johnny to come on.

He said "Jeeze, I love the cowboys," as he rubbed his hands together.

I was thinking of the way she looked at him and replied "I love the Indians more."

Johnny knew what I meant and said "I do too but the

30

cowboys are the top dogs; you can't beat the top man."

I said "hah," and hoisted my bag by throwing my shoulders in the air. We walked in close silence until we reached the Cross. The corner boys were holding up Declan the draper's. They were grown men but everybody called them corner boys. They spent long hours leaning against the brown wall, smoking and spitting and watching. I stopped to part with Johnny. "Well, there's no going back after today, so what time will you be starting out?" I asked.

"Ah, now, my father always likes the early start," Johnny answered looking up the Rock. High Street was the proper name for it but everyone but the law and the clergy called it the Rock. There is a song called "Barr na Sráide" by Sigerson Clifford about it:

O the town it climbs the mountain
and looks upon the sea,

And sleeping time or waking 'tis
there I long to be.

I thought early meant eight and laughed out loud when Johnny said ten o'clock. I nearly caused the corner boys to wake up. "I'll be up for you at half nine," I said, one eye on the girl going down my way.

"Right, good luck," Johnny put his palm up in salute and ran across the street without looking left or right. I watched him safely across and then turned down Old Market Street. The two fisherwomen were finishing for the night, carrying the box of unsold fish down from the Cross. They lived in two slate-roofed houses. The houses were old from the days of the half door. One of the women, Mary, had a brother who owned a trawler. Everyone called her Mary, from kids to canons. I often went on messages for her. She gave me a handful of apples and called me an obliging boy. She even told my mother who looked it up in the dictionary in case it had two meanings. It had but one and by the way she shook her head I knew it wasn't me. I stopped at the tap to wash the signs of blood from my hands. The tap was common to the row of dwellings

31

around Old Market Street. They had to draw water in buckets. An old woman walked out of a faded green doorway, making the sign of the cross with one hand. She wore a long dress down to her ankles. It was patterned with flowers. Flowers that had died in dirt. She was half blind so she had to feel her way through life now.

Two boys were playing handball against a garage door with a tennis ball. They were arguing nearly every shot. One of them was shouting, making fun of the other. "You wouldn't know a butt from a Gold Flake." He wanted me to hear his joke because he repeated it as I passed. A butt was when the ball hit the base line between the door and the ground. The Gold Flake was a fag butt. I knew that.

I raised my walk past the old graveyard. There were tombs with iron clasps on the stone doors. A skull had been found a few years back. People didn't pass it in the dark much after that.

I often played in the old church tower. It reared up just inside the wall, outjutting the trees. She was hurrying by the tower like a shadow thrown from the night. I aimed to pass her by the ESB pole at Bawnies Field, on the bend to the Marian. I lived in one of the house called the Ring. Four houses facing two to two with a couple of cottages completing the circle. The Ring was the white concrete road with a kerb running around it. Inside the kerb was thick grass which was criss-crossed with a narrow footpath and another square of concrete at the centre. There was just enough earth in the square to set a plant. It became known as the round square. The ESB light threw an arc inside the fence, the grass gleamed, growing out of the night. Outside on a spread of sand two boys were playing marbles, an intense air about their bent heads. The silence of the night splintered solidly as the marbles cracked into the ring. When the light heightened the colour of her hair I was half running. Her little sister nudged her as I went by and her pale cheeks reddened. Looking straight ahead I went to say "hello" but couldn't. Outside the door Patches met me.

"I'll be killed over you," he bellowed as I turned in the footpath. I shushed him and sat on the step with him, exchanging the tale. I felt better for telling him and his face lost the puckered look he was wearing.

"He's a right thorny wire," he said when I told about being struck. I ruffled his hard hair and laughed.

"You're a bit thorny yourself, kicking Johnny."

My mother banged the window for me to come in, drawing the curtain as she took one last peep out. She often sat by the side of the curtain when second Mass was over on a Sunday.

"I'm having a peep," she'd say, the unread paper on her lap.

Breda was setting the table while my mother was putting the eggs in the warmer. When my father boiled an egg he didn't use the saucepan but put it in a Batchelor's peas can.

I threw my schoolbag inside the sofa and went out the back to cut a bucket of turf. I picked out the hard black sods and chopped them with a slasher. Black burned better than the soft white turf. Patches filled the bucket as I cut, talking thirteen to the dozen about climbing Beenatee. He kept asking me to go, offering me a *Hotspur* and the latest *Dandy*. I said "no" so many times that when he offered a *Beano Annual* I refused. I didn't mean "no" to the annual but he only got it on a swap so he couldn't give it away anyway.

I finished my tea before my father came home. He smelled of stale milk. Sometimes he smelled of cows and I liked that. He had four boiled eggs for his tea and two squares of yellow meal bread. He called the bread caudy. He had a fierce appetite and my mother said "get up before the table kicks you."

He read the paper after tea under the bulb. There was no Rosary, it was the Men's Confraternity. I was too young to go there. The Secondary boys went. They wore long trousers. I had a game of marbles with Patches on the floor. There was a small hole in the concrete near the sofa and we took turns trying to hole the marbles. I won.

I fed Carlow shop bread and milk, watching him let back his ears to it. Taking the lamp from the bike I put him to bed in the turf shed. The night air swept cold as I stood in the yard, listening to the sounds coming from the night. A pair of beagles coursing the hill towards Letter. A girl's voice was reckoning out a hunt to choose the person who would be chaser. "Ink ank under the bank, ink ank out." The green hedge rustling over the doctors field. A door slamming in the echo of a woman's goodbye. I stood smelling the burned furze that blackened Beenatee, thinking of a camp fire and the way of the free wind.

I went in and stood at the kitchen door looking at Patches, Breda and my mother. Patches stretched on the sofa, his head stuck in a comic. Breda talking about the nuns to my mother, who was poking the range, raising sparks and rising Breda.

"See Breda, there's money on the way to the house." She meant the shower going up the chimney.

"Mammy that's superstitious," Breda's shocked voice informed.

"I don't care a damn if it's counterfeit," my mother laughed.

Something in her face died when she looked up and saw me.

"Who stole your jam?" she asked and I wondered what touched my face. My throat ached and I said "nothing" without looking at her. Neither Patches nor Breda saw and I closed the door. Taking my schoolbag out I tore a page from my English exercise book and finally found my italic nib at the bottom of the bag. I went to the table and took the bottle of blue ink from the back window. Shielding the page with my hand I wrote:

"Dear Mam and Dad and Breda and Pat,"

I made a paragraph.

"I'm going on a journey with Johnny. I do not know if I ever will come home again so goodbye."

Before signing it I looked at the blue shine on the page. I thought Johnny's name would help the Guard to find me. When I was crumbling the page the ink blobbed like the blue water overflowing inside me.

Asking my mother for cocoa when it was not yet nine had her firing questions by the new time. I said I wanted to be up early to go for worms along the strand.

"May God give you sense, boy," she ruffled the back of my hair.

I climbed the stairs alone. Patches stayed put, curled in a ball. I knelt on the cold lino of the bedroom floor for a long time, my mind mad with misery. In bed I tucked up to warm bringing my knees to my chin. I heard my father come in and his quick step on the stairs. I pretended to be asleep when he opened the door. I heard him tiptoe to the side of the bed and his hand came down on my shoulder. I wanted to turn from the wall but stilled my body while he tucked the bedspread round my shoulders. He left the room without a word and my body eased. Sleep came late and my dreams were green with the forest that towered over the night.

Chapter Four

Morning broke over Beenatee, searching slowly westward. The town would come to life at ten when the farmers' wives drove in for the week's messages by horse and hackney car. The hardy walked; some stayed for confession and devotions in the evening. The men spent the holy hour in the bars. The shops stayed open late. The Irish House didn't close until ten o'clock.

I heard the front door bang and the freewheel of a bike. My father; ten to nine. Hearing Patches move in his sleep next to me made me get out the bottom of the bed. I didn't want to cross over him but he was awake anyway. He watched me without a word as I said my morning prayers. He still didn't speak when I'd finished; his eyes just followed me. Without looking at him I went to wash the sleep from my eyes in the bathroom. Porridge and a cut of shop bread for breakfast. My mother asked was I better and I said that I was never worse to be well. Hospital requests were on the radio and she said I should have a song played.

The lame postman banged on the knocker and my mother dropped the poker she'd been using to quicken the fire. I heard him at the door. "Soft morning mam." He called every woman "mam." He'd no mother so I thought he wanted every woman to be his mam. "Soft morning,"—that meant the mountain mist was falling. I jumped to the window but the Ring was rainless. The morning looked quiet, the sky sombre, the grass grounded.

The door pulled shut and the postman peered at the next letter, then doubled back to deliver the letter that came with the parcel. I watched as he pulled his bad leg heavily behind him. Turning from the window I passed by my mother at the kitchen door.

"There's a letter too," I said by way of explaining.

"The poor man's doting," she said shaking her head above the parcel on the floor. I picked the letter up by the head of the Queen and took it to the table.

My mother was trying to untie the knot on the twine, eventually getting her teeth to it. Losing patience she went to the scullery for the scissors. The parcel was full of girl's clothes. I helped her pull them out. There was a strong English smell from them; moth balls. It was nice but it was a girl's smell so I pretended to hold my nose. My mother said "you smell like that yourself on a Saturday night after your bath."

I unclasped my nose and without thinking blurted out "not this Saturday night." She answered "We'll see about that anon, son," and I laughed. After she had taken the last blouse out, the brown paper lay dog-eared on the tiles. My mother put a hand on my stooped shoulder to raise herself up, saying with weight in her voice, "I'm putting on age. Finish your breakfast and throw the wrapping in the bin for me," she added, "I must have a cup of Barry's myself."

I gathered the paper up and threw it in the big bin. I rolled the white twine and put it in my pocket. My mother was pouring her tea and asked, "Do you want me to freshen it for you? It must be stone cold by now."

I said "Fill it up again Mrs Dempsey" and she poured it like a barmaid. The tea was strong.

"Well drawn," she said supping from the rim of the cup.

"Can I take Carlow for a walk?" I asked.

"'Tisn't a walk he needs but a wash in the river," she allowed.

I nearly said I'd be going nowhere near a river when I remembered I was supposed to go to Bosses strand for worms.

After breakfast my mother put on her blue coat and matching scarf. She was off to Jim Curran's for the messages. She looked different when she was dressed for uptown, powdering cheeks and nose with one hand and giving orders to the risen Patches with the other. She looked like a Guard directing traffic outside the football field, only they pulled instead of powdered their noses. I helped Patches find his socks; they were on him. While my mother slipped out the

37

door I dished out his porridge. Then I opened the porch door and walked into the morning. Sniffing the air I caught a whiff of turf smoke rising blue into the grey sky. The air was nippy and my breath was frozen; pale like the morning. There was very little sound travelling and I could hear a motor boat down the river. When the engine died I unfastened the hasp of the turf shed and let Carlow out. He was wagging his tail and yelping with delight. I quietened him down and took the twine from my pocket. Making a loop to the measure of his neck I pulled it over his face. He wouldn't stay still and playfully caught the length of string between his teeth. Finally I tied him loosely and made a smaller loop for my hand.

Patches was at the door by the time I finished, his eyes taking all in. "You're not tying him to drown are 'ou," he asked, hands in his jeans like John Wayne.

"Don't be wet," I answered, trying to lead Carlow around the yard.

Patches was eying the new string; "Who gave that to you?" he asked, "Mam?"

"It arrived round the parcel," I answered indifferently.

"Parcel?" his eyes lit up and he hopped two-legged into the yard. "Any jumper or jeans for me?"

"No, only girls' things," I said, trying to unravel Carlow from the lead.

"Bleddy girls get everything," Patches complained. "Aren't there any men in England?"

"Uncle Christy," I said

"Hah!" Patches shook his curls, "that lanky giraffe has only a snot of a daughter; she never dried up when she was home last Summer. Wouldn't even climb the hill, thought there was a tribe of Apaches at the top. Course there's no hills in London, only in the cinemas and they're only American mountains. An ..."

I was laughing when he finished. "You're a right ol' woman yourself the way you go on."

"Anyway how do you know there aren't Indians in the hills since you've never climbed them?"

"Aw, aren't I setting out today to climb Beenatee with

Brendy," he said seriously. "Indians my head," he added glancing up. The shed halved the hill and he scanned the rim where the sky touched the summit. I turned Carlow round to face the door and led him in, giving Patches a slap of the string across the shoulders.

"Good hunting brave. Don't get scalped."

"Hah! scalped my head," he scoffed, and I shouted over my shoulder.

"That's where they chop it."

I looked at the clock: twenty five past nine. I dropped the string to go upstairs for my things. Patches was playing with Carlow when I came down. I gave him my marbles and he looked suspiciously at them before taking and rolling them to see was there any kink in them. He asked me why and I told him I'd retired from playing marbles. He didn't believe me. I said goodbye to him and tried to feel sad at leaving but couldn't. Patches ran to the door to see me off, waving, one hand still in his pocket. I waved in return and let Carlow run, dragging me too fast for my legs.

I met my mother at the Cross. She was talking to Mary and I said "hello." Mary said "hello boy." She always called me boy. She called Breda girl. You would think there was no name in the family. But she gave me a big green apple and I didn't mind.

My mother said "I thought you were off to the strand?" and I said "I am, up town and down Bridge Street."

She turned to Mary. "He always takes the long road" and Mary smiled at me, her ruddy cheeks widening.

"He's got pucks of time. The day's long, the pay's small. Isn't there a great stretch to the evenings now Mrs?" she said to my mother.

She didn't even have a name for my mother. She knew everybody in town and beyond.

My mother said, "there is indeed. Aren't the Easter eggs out in Dan's window already?"

"Ah, trust him to hatch early," Mary laughed, her chest heaving.

My mother thought she was great dust and laughed too.

"God bless now, Mrs." Mary turned to a country woman. "Fresh mackerel, nice whiting Mrs."

My mother called "So long Mary" and I walked on down with her.

"Can I have an Easter egg mam?" I pleaded, "for the road." I picked up that saying from my father at Christmas. He said he couldn't leave the Corner House until he'd one for the road. And when my mother asked was it one pint or one barrel he said, "I don't know about that but it was a long road."

That humoured her and I remembered it now. "You can have one, if it's the Paupers' road you're thinking of," she said and I laughed. The Paupers' road was short. "How much are they?" she asked poking around in her purse.

"I only want a threepenny one," I said generously. The big round ones in boxes cost half a crown but they had chocolate sweets inside the shell. She found a silver threepenny bit with the crouching rabbit on one side. The harp was on the other side.

She stopped outside Dan's and I said, "thank you mam said Dan."

"That's what he said too."

"Goodbye for now and ever, mam," I added, my face solemn.

"I'll give you ever, you little dickens" she said, not knowing I meant it. She patted Carlow and called "don't be late for dinner," and she was gone around the barber's shop at the corner. I stood a while looking against the faded yellow corner with the red and white sign hanging out above the frame of the door. It turned into Dan's, the bell ringing as I pushed open the door. It was dark within and I smelled the fresh bread on the counter. "Well boy?" Mrs Dan's tall figure developed out of the doorway, "what can I do for you?"

"A threepenny Easter egg please." I always said "please" in the shops.

"An Easter egg is it?" she said.

"It is," I said patiently.

She reached her hand out to the window and withdrew an Easter egg. It was wrapped in blue-dotted silver paper. She offered it into my hand and I put the threepenny bit in her free palm.

"Much obliged," she thanked me and popped the money in a pull-out drawer under the counter.

"So long," I said and I opened the door to let Carlow out. The bell rang again. "That divil of an Angelus is enough to make you pray."

Dan came through the kitchen door. "Hello Dan," I called and his smiling face brightened in the darkness.

"Good morning to yourself boy."

Outside the sun was beginning to show signs of gold on Carlow's back. Looking up to the Cross I saw a cyclist pedalling down the steep height from the Rock, his red head like raging fire. "Johnny," I thought. Nobody else would have the neck to pedal down from the Rock. Even freewheel was dangerous without a touch of brakes. My heart went to my mouth. He didn't have brakes on the racer. He made it himself. I started to run, then stop, opened my mouth but no sound came. He was nearing the Cross ... if a car ... I shut my eyes, heard a bell ... open again I saw him flash across and into Old Market Street. A car and a donkey's cart collided in the middle of Main Street. Brakes and hee haws squealed in the air and Mary waved a fist after Johnny. He was freewheeling now and grimly holding the bouncing bike to the little street.

"Johnny, brake with your shoe," I cried, leaping in against Dan's wall. A blur of red flashed by, followed by a rise of wind, and he was gone. I turned and ran round the barber's just in time to see an old woman's message bag disappear from her hand, hooked on the handlebars of Johnny's wild racer.

The old lady leaned against the wall of the graveyard that almost became her last resting place. I ran, letting Carlow free down to Bawnies Field. Taking the shortcut I scrambled up the height to the stone wall that led to the Terret. Jumping down the rocks to the sheer edge I was just in time to see the bike hit the iron railing along the steps of the pier and Johnny sailing in a cycling fashion into the water. I skidded down the steep path that led to the pier road. On my feet at the bottom I sprinted, my legs bouncing awkwardly off the rubber of my wellingtons.

41

A bulky man was hauling in a rope, letting it slip back through his fingers with every pull. By the time I reached the edge Johnny's plastered hair was showing. He was spluttering and crying out "I'm drownded, save me, save me," as he grasped the wet heavy rope. Finally his chest was on the edge and the man, Mary's brother, was pounding his back while the water drained from his mouth. His face turned a pale green and he vomited. I felt sick myself watching him and went over to the twisted frame of the bike. The front wheel was buckled, the handlebars twisted round the way he came. Mary's brother was still slapping away and coaxing "that's it boy, get it all up" and Johnny answering "I'll get up to you in a minute if you don't stop belting me," in a pained voice.

When I heard him speak I went over saying, "What was all that in aid of?"

Johnny blew his nose with two fingers, straightened up and answered "Me, I won ten bob on a bet that I wouldn't cross the Main Street." His blue eyes flashed with water and light.

"Ten bob wouldn't pay for your coffin," the man said, gathering up the rope and shaking his head.

"You're a crazy horse." I shook his shoulder admiring his daring.

The man turned back from the pier edge. "Did you have anything in the message bag?" he asked, pointing to a plastic bag floating out to the strong current.

"Mercy me," Johnny cupped his mouth. It was the old lady's shopping bag. "What'll we do?" he asked, looking at me.

"Get the wind up," I replied while the man shook his head again.

"Modern children," he muttered under his breath.

Chapter Five

I caught up the bike and wobbled it away.

"My blinking wheel's bent," Johnny complained forgetting about the bobbing bag.

"Do 'mind the wheel. Come on, we're supposed to be on our journey by this time."

"Let the time wait. The pony's being shod anyway," Johnny was more concerned with testing his legs for a limp.

"Oh?" I said, "we'd better be off even so." I think the Guards might be after you for this."

"The Guards," Johnny echoed. "They couldn't catch chickens ..." he paused, and I didn't think it was much of a joke ...

"Pox," he finished.

I laughed more at the pause than anything else. The pause suited the Guards. I wheeled the wreck while Johnny gathered Carlow's lead. The dog had wandered off to explore the dock.

"I'd better take the short cut home by the Avenue and get out of these rags before I catch my death of cold," Johnny spoke through his chattering teeth.

"But that takes us past the Guards' Barracks," I stopped wheeling.

"Won't I save their poor legs if they want to arrest me." He grinned, the impish mouth turned at the corners.

"You're dotty!" I said and walked on to the pier road.

"What's that in your pocket?" Johnny spied the Easter egg.

"An Easter egg I'm hatching," I smiled.

"Easter eggs at this time of year! Johnny laughed. "Aren't the turkeys still laying?"

"They are not," I answered strongly, "it's gone Christmas."

"How do the bleddy turkeys know, they haven't been

43

converted, have they?"

Johnny had forgotten his mishap.

"They're Christians in Turkey," I said lamely, adding, "that's a country."

"I know, tinkers know geography," Johnny said proudly.

He stumped me with a clever question then.

"Is Turkey a fair country or a foul country?"

"How do I know?" I said and Johnny slapped my back.

"If it's called Turkey it must be fowl."

I made a face and stopped to let the bike lean against my back while I unwrapped the silver paper.

"Here, you can have half, Johnny," I tore the chocolate and the middle pulled pink. Johnny ate his in two bites and I savoured mine. At the top of the road we twisted right along the pier road leading to the Marian. At the grotto I turned in the doctor's field, lifting the bike over the stone wall. Johnny gave me a hand. One. At the end of the path through the hayfield we came to the Avenue. Two Guard's sons, a class above us in school, were having a goal-to-goal match with a torn football. The red bladder was hanging out like guts. Nobody owned the Avenue; I thought maybe it belonged to the Guards. They spent their summer evening watching the intense street football matches being battled out before them.

Johnny asked one of the boys, the new sergeant's son, for a kick but the fellow didn't understand and turned back to his goal.

"Isn't he from Cork?" I explained to Johnny, "they only play hurling there."

"What's he doing with a fine football like that so?" Johnny kicked a round stone, releasing his disappointment.

"Getting civilised," I answered trying out a new word I heard Breda use.

Johnny responded quickly, "he's a long way to go by crikey, he isn't even civil yet."

I pushed the bike to Johnny, "Your turn," I said. Johnny took it and dropped Carlow's lead. "I've just had a turn, a bad turn!" he exclaimed.

I laughed and grabbed Carlow's lead in case he might run

out in the Main Road.

At the top of the Avenue stood the Protestant Church. I never saw anyone going up the gravel pathway to the churchyard. It was half-hidden by trees and set back from the street. Behind the Church the few fields slanted to the hill, only broken by the Old Road that ran above the town. The Old Road started from the Fair Field and went west in the old days when the town stretched, following the valley that nestled between the hills and the river.

> We sang for joy beneath the sky,
> Life held no print or plan
> And we boys in Barr na Sráide
> Hunting for the wran.

The street was quiet but for a crowd of boys outside the football field. All the top Guards lived in New Street. My father said it had something to do with the new thinking abroad. I thought it was strange that France or any other country abroad could decide that the Guards must live in New Street. Johnny turned the bike across the street to the narrow footpath by the Church. He was talking away about what he was going to buy with the ten bob he'd won. I was wondering if Patches had made a start with his expedition yet.

Mary was still at the Cross but she was making a bargain with a countrywoman. The woman had close cropped hair and wore a long shabby coat. Johnny said "hurry up or she'll slap a sale on us. A sole." I ran to keep up with him, dragging Carlow behind. Rock Street must have been the climb that made the songwriter sit down, I thought, because it climbed the mountain. Most of the houses were old but so brightly painted that they looked span new. Some of the houses still had the half-door. With the main door open the half-door was shut and often used as an arm rest by the old people who lived there. Johnny lived in the uppermost houses next to the High Field; next door to him was Banjo. It was said that with the High Field on one side and Banjo on the other, the Coffeys heard nothing but the wind out of tune with the grass. Dusty the sweep and Roll-Away Bob were the nearest neighbours. Roll-

Away was young and went on the beet to England in the winter. Come summer he'd return, dressed to kill with a clean white shirt and navy blue suit. He wore winkle picker shoes pointy enough to try a hen for eggs, as my mother remarked. His hair swam with Brylcream and was combed back to turn up over his collar. Dusty the sweep was as black as the ace of spades, even on Sunday. He was forever whistling the same tune:

> I'm a rambler, I'm a gambler,
> I'm a long way from home,
> And if you don't like me,
> Just leave me alone.
> I eat when I'm hungry,
> I drink when I'm dry,
> And if moonshine don't kill me,
> I'll live till I die.

He will too.

Halfway up I took the handlebars and Johnny pushed. Coming down on the other side was Silver. Johnny whispered even though we were a long way from him. "The hatchet man's scouting today."

I looked across out of the corner of my eye. He was a tall severe man with eyes that stared straight through you. He carried a cord message bag and shopped only once a week. He was known as Silver and even the cold hard name made me shiver. He took a hatchet to a neighbour one Christmas. The neighbour went to wish him a "happy Christmas" and was chased from his door. I never saw him at Mass. He lived alone and never went out but once a week. His was the only house in town that the Wren boys avoided.

"He should be sent to the White House," I said when he passed. The White House was the mental hospital in Killarney. There was one in America too!

I fell silent when Silver had melted from my mind. We passed the fork, stopping to watch two boys sword-fighting with a couple of sally rods. The bark had been skinned and the white skin glinted when the sun glanced off them. The boys were swaying and feinting in the middle of the road. There was little chance of cars coming up the Rock. I left them arguing about who "kilt" who first. The air was heavy with the smoke of firewood, bogdale and turf. I loved the clean smell of the turf smoke; it looked like a blue halo over the town.

We passed Banjo's house; the door was ajar but it was too dark inside to see anything. Johnny knocked on Roll-Away Bob's door. I stood on the curb of the footpath and kicked a Sweet Afton pack down an open drain. Looking over my shoulder I saw the door slip open and the black head of Roll-Away appear.

"Coffey you have the cheek of Nick himself."

I heard Johnny say "you mean Banjo" and they were laughing like loonies.

Nick was Banjo's real name. Johnny came away with a grin plastered all over his face.

Johnny kept looking at the faded red note, saying "the first ten shillings I've ever earned. Here I'll give you a half-crown," he said.

I refused. "Don't be so free. You'll need it. The rainy day you know."

"Rainy day!! It's been raining for years on me. It's a wonder I'm not called Noah." Johnny seemed upset. I laughed at the way he said "Noah," it sounded like "no way."

"Do 'mind," I calmed him. "The poor shall inherit the earth." I learned that at catechism and went home feeling like a millionaire.

"Hah!" Johnny said, "the earth between the ditches; the long hard road I'll have to follow like my father."

His voice shook a little, with cold I thought. Suddenly I felt I didn't want to join the caravans, be with the travelling people. I wanted to journey alone, but I knew not where.

"Johnny," I stopped and he stopped too. "Is it going to be alright for me, is it? I'm going to be different …" I trailed off.

"O' course it's alright nickle treasure. It's because you're different to the townies that I'm opening the door to you."

He pushed me forward by the shoulder and I was facing his closed door.

I dropped Carlow's lead and Johnny pushed the door in. The dirty concrete floor was cold even through my shoes. The front window was draped with a red curtain. I thought there were white dots on it but it was too dim inside to see.

Chapter Six

The back window was boarded up. The open fire was smoking, the turf damp. Johnny left the door open and the gloom was lit by daylight. A figure with a black shawl knelt on the hearth, pushing newspaper under the turf. I looked around the kitchen. The dresser was bare except for three cracked cups hanging on six-inch nails. Two worn armchairs slumped against the walls on each side of the fire. The coarse hair was falling from an old sofa by the front window. A table with two legs steadied with bits of plywood stood in the middle of the kitchen, making the room look small. Two closed doors led to the bedrooms; I wondered which was Johnny's. He went up to the fire and laid a hand on his mother's shoulder. She got up slowly, holding one leg, and turned her black eyes to me.

"God bless, boy," she said, just like she said when I opened the door to her at Christmas, when she was begging. I'd given her a threepenny bit out of my own pocket.

I answered "hello, Mrs Coffey," and she smiled. I'd never seen her without the narrow look before. I hoped she wouldn't remember me. If she did, she never let on, only said "You're the creamery man's boy, aren't you?"

"I am," I said and she nodded.

"He works hard the seven days, God keep him."

I said nothing but smiled a small smile as she drew her shawl around her small frame. She stood in my silence for a moment before drawing out a chair from the table. "Here boy, rest your four bones here."

"Thanks," I sat down on the edge, embarrassed.

"Johnny, have you got a spark yet?" She was shivering with cold, wrapping her long fingers round her waist.

"Nearly blazing, Missus," he said over his shoulder.

I looked up to see what her face said to "missus" but there was no blame in her eyes. I looked at the fireplace but all that could be seen was the damp smoke of the smouldering turf. While Johnny rooted stuffed paper I looked round the walls. I couldn't make out the colour but it looked yellow and dirty. A Sacred Heart picture hung by a nail over the fireplace. The exposed heart of Jesus running black with age and neglect. There was a statue of Our Lady on top of the dresser. She was alone, her arms empty of the Infant. The wall with the boarded window had the imprint of a picture frame in the dust.

I dropped my eyes quickly as Johnny got up. The fire was kindled and his mother pushed an armchair right up to the hearth. He'd left the bike outside the door and said "stay put" when I made to get up. I wanted to say "what about Carlow," but I was too shy in the house. He wheeled the bike across the kitchen and opened a door I hadn't noticed. He beckoned me out. The back yard looked like the council dump. Bits of bicycles, old coats, flashlamps, harness and pieces of rotten rope lay scattered. Johnny had kicked in the door of an old shed and was forcing the bike in.

"Give me a hand," he said and I pushed the saddle and the back wheel reared up into the air. With one more heave it rolled in and Johnny nearly fell over. "Is your mother coming with us in the caravan?" I said, looking out for a bicycle bell in the shed. I wanted to put a bell on Carlow. Johnny shook his head.

"Johnny, did you see Carlow when you went out the front for the bike?"

Johnny fingered his jaw like an old man before answering slowly, "No, I never clapped eyes on him."

I turned quickly and half-ran into the dirty dark kitchen, calling over my shoulder, "I'll see if he's there." I looked up and down the Rock Road; he was nowhere to be seen.

Johnny strolled out and I spoke before he opened his mouth. "No sign. I'll see if he found his way home."

"Will you ever come back?" Johnny put a questioning hand on my shoulder. "I'll be lost on the road without you."

"O' course I'll be back, I gave my word," I said feeling free of doubt again. I went back in to say "goodbye." His mother was

50

huddled into the crackling fire. The flames lighting up the kitchen and firing shadows on the walls. No sound came from her. She looked as if she'd never move again. I opened my mouth to say "so long" to the black figure but changed my mind. Instead I said "See you very soon" to Johnny.

He answered "Righto," his eyes troubling as he turned to go to his mother.

Outside the Rock was beginning to stir, the people at the half-doors looking half-awake. Children played football with a red rubber ball that bounced all angles on the bumpy road. Thinking of Johnny's gamble I walked carefully across the street. My mother opened the door for me and I ducked under her hand into the kitchen. Carlow was in the scullery lapping a plate of buttermilk. He stopped to look at me and wagged his tail. I watched as he drank the milk and felt hungry myself.

My mother asked "why did you send him home?"

When I told her what happened, she said, "you haven't a splink of sense to be up and down with the Coffey clan."

I asked for a cut of bread and butter and sprinkled sugar over it. I drank a cup of milk with the sweet bread. I was forbidden to take Carlow out again so I sulked out the door for the last time.

When I reached the Rock again Johnny was bargaining with Banjo over the bike. When he saw me approaching he must have made a deal because Banjo handed him some money and Johnny gave him the bike, bent wheels and all. He turned to me and laughed "mun for fun," delighted with the sale.

"Well, did you find Carlow?"

"Yes," I answered, "how much did you make?"

He showed me the two pound notes and I showed surprise.

It was hardly worth ten shillings. Banjo was blinkered.

Johnny folded the notes before sticking them down his wellington. "My father's back with the mare," he said straightening up. "He's getting a few groodles for the road. He's talking the old lady out of the journey too."

"Your mother," I corrected, not liking him calling her "the old lady."

Johnny only said "yes" and beckoned me to the field that ended the Rock. A road led out of the Rock between the scattered farms.

"The mare is grazing up the road," Johnny said by way of explaining our course.

"Has she been shod?" I said for something to say.

"Shod, she's better shod than I am," Johnny turned his right foot up. The wellington had worn away and I could see his sock..

I laughed and said "I'd like to see you with a few nails through your hoof."

"I'd be in good company. The company of Christ," he said solemnly.

"Hah! maybe the priests and brothers might even think I'm good enough for their holy houses," he added looking straight at me.

I said nothing; I'd never even asked him to call at my door. Johnny continued as if he'd not noticed my silence. "I wonder was He ever nailed to that Cross?"

"How do you think He was stuck to it, by glue?"

"No, they didn't have glue in them days," Johnny laughed.

"They didn't have six nails either," I said without thinking.

Johnny stopped walking, a puzzled look on his face and no laugh in his eyes. "Jesus," he said, "nailed to the Cross, that's what they told us! Are they codding us or what?"

"Somebody's wrong," I said and felt defeated. We walked on in a strange silence.

The pony was grazing on the tall grass that pleated the ditches. In summer the grass shimmered when a breeze skimmed the ditch. Now it lay lank in the light of a dull sky. The pony raised its head when we came close, lifting her ears and blowing through her nose. I kept my distance while Johnny touched her near flank before lifting her hind leg. The shoe was shined with silver and the hoof newly pared.

"A mighty job," Johnny said easing the hoof gently to the ground. "Smiler Smith's a topper at shoeing horses."

Johnny turned and I asked "had she a name?"

Johnny laughed shortly "No! we've not christened her yet, she's a class of pagan." He turned back to slap her rump and I smiled to myself.

The mare wandered off, following the hidden grass that grew sweet between the wild hay-stems. We turned back to the Rock and no word passed between us while we were walking to the house. I wanted to wait outside but Johnny took my shoulder and I went inside again.

"You're in no form to go anywhere, woman!" Johnny's father was setting out the tackle on the floor while the mother was tying a scarf to her head.

"I'm a true woman of the road, Axme Coffey, and I'd rather take the hard way than suffocate in this coffin cabin," she sniffed and drew her covered head above him.

"Hah! suffocate on grandeur. You should count yourself blest that you saw a bit of the high life." He threw the bridle down in answer.

"High! God above, is that why this place is called Top Street?" She raised her eyes to the black ceiling. "Well, woman, if you're not said by me this will be your last road surely?" Axme admitted defeat.

I stood listening at the door until Johnny pushed me in.

"Have you the bridle ready yet Axme?" Johnny asked his father.

I covered a smile with my hand. Axme! He took no notice of the nickname and threw the reins to Johnny. "Here," he said, "and talk some horse sense into your mother while you're at it."

The stubborn stand of the woman grew stiffer. "Tom, we've a visitor to the house." She said it quietly but I felt I was a weapon of war.

Blushing I said "I'm with Johnny" when Axme's eyes questioned me.

"Good on you, welcome to Top Street. A town boy I bet?" He looked me from head to toe.

"The creamery man's child," she explained, and Axme got to his feet.

"Go' way," he said surprised, "didn't your da pull me out of a ditch some time back?"

I smiled and he added, ruefully, "I got a bit wet the same night."

"A bit!" she said and repeated it in a disbelieving voice, "*a bit!*, Tom Coffey you were flutthered!"

"Me?" Axme repeated too, "me drunk, wasn't it the bleddy pony that capsized me?"

"And who was to blame for driving in over the ditch?" she asked, but I could tell she was teasing.

"Well woman, as I said to the sergeant awhile ago, don't ax me, ax the driver," and he bellowed with laughter.

Johnny was bursting his sides and I looked at his mother to see a smile soften the hard lines of her face. I felt at home.

The pony was tackled and backed between the wild blue shafts. I held the reins while Axme and Johnny went into the house for the last time. The pony with no name was restless, her ears pointed for the road. I felt her excitement and my heart missed a beat. After a spell Axme and Johnny came out, their faces long and alike too, I noticed. The mother stayed behind and I saw the red curtain draw back like a mouth that was torn and in the wounded window her face broke wet with pain. I looked away because her eyes might blind me with blame.

Chapter Seven

Johnny led me to the door at the back of the trap. There was an iron step to haul yourself up with. The trap had a varnished seat all the way round with a front seat across. I sat on the outside of the front seat with Johnny on the left. He looked towards the window and turned quickly away to meet my eyes. He smiled a small smile and suddenly a sad and a lost look came over his face. I smiled too, but not for Johnny. Axme climbed up the side with the reins in one hand. He never looked near the window but slapped the pony; it sounded like a door closing, forever. I looked behind his shoulder and a long hand moved in front of the face that was framed for always in my memory. I would look back and pretend I was waving goodbye to my own mother. The trap had rubber wheels and bounded silently over the road. Axme broke the two silences between him. He turned an eye on me and said "Johnny tells me ye're great friends?"

"We're blood brothers," I answered seriously and he clapped me on the shoulder, one hand driving the pony. I thought, "It's no wonder he goes in over ditches." His coat showed a tear under the arm when he raised it. A musty smell came from him and his boots were brown from dried mud.

"Blood brudders, is it?" "Well I suppose it's the best way to be this weather," he said.

The Angelus bell sounded in another silence and three hands blessed.

"The time is good, thank God," Axme said after the Angelus.

"We won't bother with the Rocky Road to Dublin," he added as he pointed the pony down by the Fair Field. We passed the Secondary school on the right; opposite was the white walled front of the courthouse.

"Do you clever boys know the difference between those two

55

buildings?" Axme asked.

"No," we both said without effort.

"Well." He always said "well." I thought he was either wet or deep … "One is the right lesson and one is the wrong answer and which is which I don't know." There was no answer to that from either of us.

Once clear of the cluster of houses along Carhan Road I felt free. At the horse's well the pony shot across the road to drink. I often drank from it myself when I was returning from a long day at the races. Axme was saluting everyone that passed, be it bike, horse or car. He gave the priest's salute to the walking figure of a man who dressed like a priest. He was called Father Foola and he travelled all over the country. I once heard a Secondary boy say "he was a true foot soldier of Christ." They learned about Caesar at the Secondary school. Father Foola doffed his black hat and a grey tangle of hair fell over his brow.

Johnny made fun of him; "I'd hate to get any penance from him. Instead of six Our Fathers he'd give you six miles of meditation."

"Now, now, Johnny, he may not be the full shilling but he's as harmless as the day's long," Axme said.

"Isn't it dark at six?" Johnny replied quickly and Axme threw me a raised eyebrow.

"The country's gone haywire with education," Axme said sadly.

I laughed and winked across at the cheeky look on Johnnie's face.

I looked away left to the shallow river. The tide was going out; on a long journey like me. But it would return to the shore. And I? The Railway bridge slanted a black shadow across the water. Knocknadobar, the mountain with the Stations of the Cross, stood bare in the grey light. The middle cross at the highest point stood still, like death against the sky. I couldn't see the two crosses on either side without climbing the hill. The fourteen stations were staked to the hill in a winding way to escape the outcrop of rock and incline. Incline to the sky … God … I felt. He watched from the valley between the mountain and the sky. People said "incline to rain," about the

56

weather. Incline to the sky, near God. I felt close to the mountain; it would never change. People were different; even I would change, grow and learn, go out to touch the world, be touched. I didn't know but I was on my way even now.

Johnny and Axme were talking about the old lady left behind. I heard their voices but my mind wasn't listening. We passed the Primrose Road. Long ago the poor people walked it, on their way to the market that the town grew from. I could close my eyes and see them with bags and baskets. The women dressed in drab shawls, the men in knitted Arans. Their bare feet making slow footprints in the summer dust.

The road grew wide and swept around in a half circle. The pony must have sensed something; she picked up the slack reins and trotted in double echoes off the road. Axme lost the reins and lost his voice in dark words. I pretended not to hear; my father didn't abide bad words.

"Ah, well, boys, the wild west's round the next corner."

Axme gave the pony head and laughed with his head thrown back. The three of us were laughing as the road dipped down to the yellow and black stripes of the bridge. The main road tightened left across the bridge. A country road to Carhan followed the river towards the wood. I could step across the water by the rocks at low tide. In the summer of olden days open air dances were held by the side of that road. The Rocky Road started on the Famine Mound. In a clearing I could see the green canvas of a caravan. For a moment I felt unreal, a projection of the pictures. The covered wagon and I, the naked Indian, both afraid. A car came over the bridge sweeping wide at the cross. A face behind owlish glasses looked up at the trap. It looked like the vet's car.

At the front of the caravan a big man stood, legs apart, watching our arrival. His hair was high and red, his bare brown arms covered in tattoos. I felt my stomach sumersault as his narrowed eyes gripped my face. They were blue and harder than any winter sky.

"Jacko!" Johnny shouted and waved wildly, standing up on the trap. Jacko's eyes widened and he took two steps to catch the bridle and bring the pony to a halt. He reached out his arms and picked Johnny from the trap. The tattoos on his arms took to life. My mouth must have opened in awe because Axme layed a hand on my head. "He's mean strong, that bucko."

Jacko was swinging Johnny up and down, then he just pushed upwards and Johnny shot into the air. I closed my mouth to catch my breath. He caught Johnny by the ankles on the way down and held him aloft before lowering him to the ground. Axme winked at me and got down from the trap. He put up his thin arms to receive me to the ground.

"I never dreamt you'd the two sons Axme?" Jacko was looking at me and I looked at Axme and back to Jacko to catch him smiling. I thought his smile was a test and I half-smiled in return.

"An' how would you like a heave boy?" he spoke to me in a soft voice.

I looked at my feet, looked at Johnny's eager face.

Axme broke in "leave the lad on the road. Isn't there enough air down here?"

"I suppose he's windy enough as it is?" Jacko said, a little harder than before.

I could feel the hot colour course through my cheeks. I looked straight at Jacko. A test. "I'm not afriad. You can heave me if you care to."

I stood my ground, tightening my shoulders as his giant hands clasped them. He cleaned me from the ground with one sweep. I smelled the stain of sweat under his arms. He brought me level with his eyes before steadying himself. My heart hammered against my chest, my mouth drained dry. For a moment I lived outside myself, in the air, free. Then falling forever, eyes tight until Jacko gripped my ankles and balanced me upright. I opened my eyes and looked down. The road looked a long way but Jacko was smiling and the smile was mine this time. When my feet touched the rutted road I let my breath explode. Johnny clapped me on the back and Axme said "fair play to you boy."

Jacko added "a true son of the travelling people" and I felt proud to burst.

"He wants to travel the single ticket with us," Axme

explained my presence.

Jacko cupped his chin and looked doubtfully at me.

"And what put that notion into you head?" he asked.

"Johnny and ..." I trailed off. "We're brothers, blood-brothers," I said bravely.

"Ah Jesus Geronimo! We're not bleddy film stars," Jacko threw his arms in the air to match his heightened voice.

He turned on Axme. "You haven't a splink. What's his parents going to do? Let him gallivant to Galway?"

"Well, there might be worse places if I could think of any," Axme was listening with a laugh.

"I can, Mountjoy prison where we'll all come to journey's end, for kidnapping," Jacko put pain in his voice.

"Kidnapping," he repeated to me but I said "I can't kidnap myself ... if I don't mind."

"Mind!" Jacko made great use of the one word I noticed. "What mind? You haven't a mind between the two of you," he paused looking at Johnny, "nor maybe the three of you."

Johnnie's face flashed back at him.

"That's the reason he, we want to go' way, from people making little. The Brothers, the Guards, the big shots, the bastards," Johnny swore and I turned, not believing I heard right. "And now you, blow you!" Johnny ran out of breath.

Jacko lowered his voice.

"Calm yourself Johnny, I'm not making little of anyone, I'm only making sense. But," he turned his brittle blue eyes on me, "if the boy wants to go, give him the road."

I didn't break my gaze looking back at him and he accepted my silence, saying "don't renege on us." I made no reply.

The caravan stood facing the bridge, two blocks of concrete under the front wheels. Johnny led round the back and I felt Jacko's gaze follow me in turn. I could smell the blue paint from the shafts, carrying clear on the wind. With the green gleam of the canvas rising into a sudden patch of blue sky my mind took on the colour of the home that would always be a dream. Johnny was talking, praising Jacko to the sky; I was only half listening. I heard a voice salute Johnny. I looked up to see a women with a gold flame of hair swing from the steps of the caravan. She wore a red skirt with a blue shawl on her shoulders. She stepped down backwards and turned to shake Johnnie's two hands. Her face faded with freckles, faded further when she saw me. Her smile for Johnny was transfixed as if she couldn't wipe the welcome from her face. I said a small "hello" and she returned a short answer. Johnny whispered a few words in her ear and her face came to rest.

Chapter Eight

The day was picking up, the clouds breaking and sweeping to the Atlantic, leaving the sky a patchwork of blue. The sun played on Carhan wood, touching the distant dark of the trees to a green light. The brightness picked out the ridges of ditches that divided Beenatee into fields of furze. The wind had fallen silent and the furze had softened on the hill.

After circling the caravan, Johnny and I went across to sit on Carhan bridge, looking into the spring flow. Axme and Jacko were harnessing the pony to the caravan and securing the trap to the back. The woman with the flame of gold hair lit a fire, feeding it twigs and bits of bogdale. She planked a black kettle on the blaze. Johnny told me she was Jacko's woman and I wondered why he didn't say wife.

Johnny was dropping gravel into the water while I stared out over the river following its left curve that took it all the way past the farm I had lived on until I was five. It was strange how I feared water since my father tried to force me to swim, feared the cold current carrying me away from the bank. The river bordered the farm. I had to go down the bog road, down the steps of the small bog to come to two fields of coarse grass that was never green. The farm wasn't ours; I knew that now but believed it belonged to my father when I was young. It was owned by a man from town. A tight-faced man with a hat and a bicycle. I remembered him shouting "get off the hay," as I played at sliding down the haycocks. I wondered would I want to return home tomorrow, like the first time in town. Saturday: setting out into the young morning to walk the three miles back to the farm, looking for home at five. I never even reached the East end of town as my big sister cycled out to stop me.

A bellow from Axme brought me mind back to the day.

Johnny left a fistful of gravel fall, making white islands on the water. I had a race back to the caravan with Johnny. I waited while the woman poured strong tea into five tin mugs. The pony was champing on the silver bit, ready for the road. Jacko squatted down to drink his tea and Axme followed suit. Johnny sat next to Jacko and I let myself down between Johnny and Axme. The woman handed me the mug and I said "thanks." She went into the caravan and returned with a square of white bread. I took only a cut out of manners but was glad when I bit into it. Tea in the air had a different taste and I took another cup when it was offered. Nobody said grace but when we all finished, Axme took off his cap and made the sign of the cross. Jacko got up and said something to the woman. She started to kick out the embers with her brown bootees. Johnny helped her, using one wellington. The flattened fire was a black patch that threw off a shadow of smoke.

Jacko surprised me by giving me a hand up to the front of the caravan. The woman and Johnny climbed up the back steps and Axme jumped up to take the reins. Jacko led the pony by the bridle, guiding her onto the even road. When the pony took the weight of the caravan she faltered but coaxed by Jacko she pulled it with her neck straining. Jacko hopped up as the pony found her stride. Taking the reins from Axme he turned her over the bridge. The four of us on the front seat, sitting tightly together. The woman in the green gloom of the caravan, behind us.

Axme touched my shoulder "I suppose you never had a spin on a tinker's truck before?"

"No, I never had," I answered regretfully and he smiled.

He had a black gap between his two front teeth. No more was said to me but now and then Johnny would glance across at his father and give me a wink. Jacko and Axme were talking; Axme in a rich run of words and Jacko in a sentence of sounds that only formed the rare word. I watched the slow ditch passing and listened to Axme name the camping sites; calling names to the farmers who hunted away the tinkers from their land. He could give the dates and days of the fairs throughout the country. I let my mind roam to the places that spun from his voice. Found wonder in the strange names and excitement in the nearness of the night.

Very little traffic disturbed the road. We met only one old man driving two cows across the road when we got to the mile sign from town. The fields were the fields of winter, grey-grassed and cold. Stretches of land hardly more than a slough, where only bullocks would graze, lay flat to the right. Between the road and the river short green fields became fertile. Small farms where the tilly lamp still shone, across the slough huddled in the distant foothills. The Paupers Road pointed in pain to the old Workhouse. We passed the ESB station or the turf station as my father called it. The electricity was powered by burning turf and my father sold a lorryfull to the station every summer.

Every summer the day at the bog. My mother packing the bread and ham, the cups and the kettle. Breda and I lugging the message bag, a strap each, without a bad word between us. My father loading my uncle's horse rails with a sleán and two turf pikes. Patches standing on tiptoe, holding the horses head.

The wind burning across the slough. The sun heavy in the sky at noon. The taste of tea in the bog, a strong memory. Nothing could blot that wild clear taste, the essence of sun stirred by the wind.

The bare brown arm of my father glistening on the slean. Our next door neighbour, Ned, giving my father a day. Always the man picking the heavy wet sods that the sleán skinned. My uncle, Mike, who lived beyond the old Workhouse, spreading the turf easily, without taking his shirt off.

The following week we'd be at Mike's bog with my father who was returning the day. The journey back, tired and happy in what my mother called the heel of the evening. I thought it was seven o'clock. We all went back in a week if the weather held. Spending a back-breaking day footing the turf. My father would take me out on the bike in the evening to finish the footing. Sometimes the midges would drive us home and we'd make two evenings of the job.

The following week we'd be at Mike's … The day I'd never see again. I felt a tightening in my throat at the thought. The road ahead suddenly stretched long and cold. I made to get up but felt weak with want.

Chapter Nine

Axme and Jacko were still talking, Johnny was driving the pony with his tongue in the roof of his mouth. Corner boys made that sound too, at girls' legs. The woman and I remained silent. I wondered was she thinking too as she didn't make a breath of noise. In no time we made the long haul to Kells station. The road levelled off as we came round by the quarry. The seafields lay calm below the road. Above the road the immobile mountain broken only by the railway track running alongside the road. Two lorries couldn't pass on parts of the road without the drivers looking out the windows to measure the inches. In another half mile we had the mountain above and the dangerous drop to the sea below. Only a stone wall the height of a man's knees to blunt a fall.

It was at the Viaduct I heard the car hooter. The railway line ran over the high span.

Axme shouted "pull in the pony, some soul is in a mad tear."

Jacko twisted the pony close to the cliff. I poked my head out the side of the caravan and on seeing "Garda" on the roof of a black car ducked back in again. The Garda car passed by slowly, the big thick frame of Guard Moran hunched over the wheel. Axme turned his face away but Johnny and Jacko looked straight ahead. The droll face of the sergeant looked out the back window. I saw him staring but couldn't read his face. "Lonesome Christmas," my mother called him more in pity than blame. My heart started to pound as the squad car crawled along.

"It's game ball for us now," Axme said finally.

The sergeant pressed his face to the back window then he abruptly turned back into the car, folding his arms in some satisfaction. Silently we all watched as the car revved up and climbed the height from under the viaduct.

Axme was the first to burst out laughing. "Bedad he must have thought you were a tinker too."

"He must have thought I was your boy," I said innocently, and Jacko slapped Axme's shoulder.

I settled down to silence again and the road took us long into the day. At Mountain Stage we stopped for water at the shop. The light was beginning to weaken, the early evening of April falling as night at six. Jacko and Axme had decided to stop for the night at a width of road beyond Glenbeigh. The village was deserted as the caravan rolled through its one straight street.

My stomach started to rumble with hunger and the thought of Saturday night sausages at home made my mouth water. Johnny put voice to my feeling by complaining "I'm starved with the hunger." Even his voice sounded weak. "'Twont be long before the kettle is rising on the fire now boys," Axme said.

"The best singing for a hungry soul," Jacko added.

He urged the pony into the half light. The pony, sensing a home, broke into a token trot. Round one more bend, the road curved wide, a clearing on either side. Jacko reined the pony into the shelter of an outcrop of rocks. Without being asked, the woman handed Jacko a cannister of water, over my shoulder. Jacko jumped down and held the cannister up for the pony. She drank spluttering and snorting and spilling some of the water. Johnny was lifted down by Jacko when the pony was done with. Axme took me to the dark ground last. Johnny and I were sent to gather firewood. We walked closely along the roadside, eyes peeled.

Johnny asked "are you a' right?"

I said "yes" and picked up a stick.

I got most of the firewood by breaking branches from a ditch. The woman took charge of the fire while Axme and Jacko unharnessed the pony.

The fire reddened quickly and the smoke rose to mingle with the fallen night. The deepening darkness had bound the broken hills, below the road, into one stark horizon. Somewhere between the fireside and the foothills a green valley was lost to the night. Above the road I could make out the jagged jut of the rocks; behind and before me the road, past and future.

A thick grey blanket was laid by the fire. I got the same mug as before for my tea. We had cold bread and cheese. Galtee. The same name as mountains. My teeth had to do some climbing too, to claim a bite. I drank two mugs of tea and felt full and warm when the woman collected the ware for washing. I lay back on my elbow watching the sparks fly into the air. Johnny sat cross-legged by Jacko listening to Axme related some "yarn of yore" as he put it. Plans for tomorrow: going back on the road to the village for first Mass. After breakfast tackling the pony to journey to Killarney. There, meeting the big cover of caravans that was the Coffey clan.

The plans made, the mugs washed, the fire warm and Jacko with his banjo.

> "I'm a free born man of the travelling people,
> Got no fixed abode, with nomads I am numbered,
> Country lanes and byways are always my ways,
> I've never fancied being lumbered."

Axme singing out of tune, Johnny la-la-ing and I clapping. The woman breaking a silent day with a smile. I forgot everything in the happy hours of music. Jacko's face softening in the firelight as he sang "She Moved Through The Fair." Something unspoken passed between the woman and he; a trembling smile played round her lips. I was watching and thought it was the wind on the fire. But, when she raised her head into a shadow, the smile a sad far-away thought was still set on her lips. I knew then why they didn't have to speak to understand. Earlier when she handed him the cannister of water she must have known without a word from him.

> "And then she went homeward with one star awake,
> As the swan in the evening moved over the lake."

The night grew darker and in it the fire became a deeper definition. It lighted the loneliness of the solitary hill. Warmed the vigil of the evening star that showed late for its time. I felt my eyes closing. Jacko was playing something sad and soft. Still. Like a forest after rain. The music rising and crying to the sky only to be blown back as rains upon the earth. I felt myself being picked up.

The music had stopped. The fire fell to ashes in the clearing of night. I stirred in my sleep. The sky was no more. The mountains had drifted away. But the smile was there, there on the face of the woman with the flame of gold for hair. Flickering in the soft candlelight thrown from a seashell, on a tea-chest. She was wearing a wrap of blue, her eyes, dark, shining into mine, smiling sadly. I pushed open my eye-lids and smiled silently back. She touched my cheek and I drifted with the mountains into the happiest dream of my life.

I was deep in a summer forest. Early morning. The sun was rising, flowing from tree to tree. The green light changing with the colours of forest life. The birds were free of the tree tops. A red squirrel flashed before my eyes. I was following a footpath, looking for a clearing. Home. My parents were waiting for me to return with Patches. I had searched from dusk to dawn, called his name in the night, until I could call no more. Lost myself to find him. And losing myself, forgot his name. Climbed a tree when morning broke and saw the gold thread. Leading into the endless forest, from the next tree. I thought it was a shaft of sun but it was too thin. I fell to the floor of the forest. Ran to the threaded tree and touched the line of gold. It held no feeling, no touch could take it, but it was there. I followed. Over the forest stream, through late grass and brambles, for miles. Losing and finding my golden way until I looked through a burn of nettles and tore through a ditch of briars. In the clearing one tree stood, and curled up against the trunk was Patches, fast asleep. I stood over him, my clothes in rags, my shoes falling off my feet, my hands red raw. My presence woke him and he uncurled his hands from his head. Clasped in his right hand was a yellow reel of thread. I looked at the reel, following the line back from where I'd come. Looked at my hand, my fingers without, feeling. Afraid my hand was dead. I reached out for the reel and Patches placed it in my palm. I felt it, held it to me as if I couldn't believe I found the beginning and finding it, found Patches. I gave him my hand and he got to his stand. Together we walked onward from the clearing, looking for our parents. The sun said noon when we found them, hand in hand. But their faces faded in the sun. We stopped and looked at each other. Without a word we ran again and the woman with the flame of gold ran as well, with Jacko at her side. Her arms closed about me and I mumbled against her hair "I'm home mammy, I'm home and I found Pat."

"We've found you too," she whispered hugging me to her heart.

Patches was being held by a kneeling Jacko.

"Don't ever lose the gold thread, father." Patches called him father and I wondered and woke.

Chapter Ten

Voices breaking over a Sunday silence. A car door slammed, the angry echo bouncing across the valley, the dawn valley. Still in the cold air, as if the fields were frozen. The mountains separating softly in the grey light. I opened my eyes but the caravan was filled with night. I had the strange image of the dream clinging to my mind and I called Patches's name. Johnny answered me from the darkness, "the Guards, be quiet." My heart took off and I pressed a hand to my chest to muffle the sound. At the top of the caravan the tall shape of Jacko was crouching, looking through the flap of the canvas. Axme was asleep at the back so Johnny and I must have been in the middle.

I heard the official voice, clear and grey as the morning air.

"This is the sergeant outside ..." I lost the end of his sentence because the awakened Axme whispered from the back.

"Now there's a man who know's where he is."

I heard Johnny snigger through his nose.

Jacko was answering the sergeant "I haven't set eyes on a boy or a child."

"How many is within the caravan?" the sergeant pursued.

"Six, including two goats," Jacko answered lightly.

"I'm not interested in goats," the sergeant bleated.

"Ah, of course not, it's only the kid you're after." Jacko was rising him.

Axme clutched his sides laughing, "I don't think the sergeant copped onto that one." He didn't.

"Yes," he said. "We want the boy and we have grave reason to believe he's with the caravan." He lowered his voice to mark the word 'grave'. Just like the Canon, I thought.

Jacko didn't answer for a time, just glanced in my dark

69

direction. "Well, sergeant, I don't know where you get your reasoning from but you've arrived at the wrong door."

"I see," the sergeant said, "well an' good. I won't bother you any more, but if you happen on a boy along your road, leave a message at the nearest barracks."

"I certainly will, Sergeant. What does he look like?" Jacko was politeness itself.

"Look like?" the sergeant repeated. "Oh, just a boy, about ten, curly hair, foxy, with freckles. A friend of Johnny Coffey's I'm assured."

"Is he now, sure if you're assured, he must be some class of friend." Jacko was rising the sergeant to the rafters.

"Well, good day to you," the sergeant turned away and we all burst into quiet laughter.

"Good morning," Jacko called, his face caught in the flap of light.

They all looked at me, even the woman whom I hadn't seen stirring. I was silent, silent and cold. The morning air was sharp and I shivered. Hunger wormed at my stomach. I wanted to go to the lav. I held my silence like a shield. The squad car started up. They all looked away. Listening.

The woman scrambled out the back of the caravan. She was dressed in the blue shawl and her clothes were rumpled. Jacko lit the candle and his face shone, black with whiskers. Axme cleared his throat and Johnny reached across to squeeze my shoulder. I smiled, a small tired smile and waited for Jacko to speak. He stepped slowly over and knelt on one knee beside me.

"Listen to me." I listened, my eyes half-closed. "I can find no fault in you. You seem a nice quiet boy. No trouble, except the bother we'll be in if you're found with us. And ..." he paused "that's why you must return. If you were related it would be bad enough but you're a settler's son and ..." he shrugged his shoulders.

I looked into his face, pleading with my eyes. I turned to Axme; he was lying down again. Finally I spoke and addressed myself to Johnny. "If you don't want me to stay I'll go back, Johnny."

He looked to Jacko first and I tried to catch the message, but in vain. "O' course I want you to stop. I asked you to travel, but Jacko is the caravan man."

I didn't answer Johnny but turned my eyes to Jacko. I couldn't think what to say. There was a stinging in my mind. The night came back to me. The music. The dream. The dawn. The night came back and gave no answer.

I answered and the answer I gave changed me. Gave me a longing for the rest of my life. A longing for the home built in the dream of the night. "I'll go home," I said simply, knowing they'd be no rest inside me.

"I know," Jacko said.

Johnny threw an arm round my shoulder "Maybe when you're old enough you can 'follow'."

Axme got up on one elbow and shook his head. "It's fright altogether when the boy's heart was set."

"His heart will always travel if he sets it on the stars," Jacko said softly. Strange. I almost understood the meaning of the night.

The woman called something from outside and we all got up, following Jacko. I had slept in my clothes and brushed myself with my hands. Jacko and Johnny were first into the morning. Axme was yawning as he lifted me to the ground. A hot mug of tea to warm my hands with. I stooped on one knee resting a thick slice of bread on my thigh. The smell of burning firewood was wafting across the valley. Jacko told Axme they'd take me back to the village to Mass and the Guards could take me home. The woman was openly staring at me and looked away when I raised my eyes. The sky was bursting with cloud and I could taste the rain on the wind. The fire blew squalls of smoke into the rocks when the wind caught the flame. I felt like the colour of the morning, like the sun had set in the east.

The pony was fed, her head tied into a bag of oats with a white enamel bucket of water to drink. I stood and watched while the pony was tackled. Saw the hollow day deepen across the hollow hills. Empty. The valley was bare, the stream that gave it life looked frozen. The sapling forest above the road swayed weakly on the strength of the rising wind.

71

Johnny joined me when the pony was ready for the road. He put his arm round my shoulders. "I wish you were going on with us, nickle treasure."

I put my hand on his shoulder. "That's my only wish too, Johnny I ..."

Jacko put the full stop on my unfinished sentence. "We're off," he shouted, and with our arms around each other Johnny and I moved nearer to goodbye. The woman came out of the caravan to see me off. Her hair shone; even in the early light it was a flame of gold. The blue wrap across her shoulders was closed at the front with one hand. She said no word of farewell, only raised her free hand, palm upward, like peace. I looked back before Jacko turned the pony to the road. She smiled, the night smile, her sad, sad smile and I waved once before turning my eyes homeward.

Only the soft sound of the wheels on the road. The cut of the wind as it broke over the light trap. The jingle of the harness in time to the trot of the skittish pony. Time. I wanted to know the hour. Caught Johnny's eye and pointed to my wrist. He whispered to Axme. Twenty to eight: time for first Mass. I never went to first, always to half nine. I'd forgotten to say my morning prayers, and nights, my night. I made a hidden sign of the cross, half turning my back. I formed the words to make them real. In my mind I framed the picture of the boy Jesus who left his father's house, like me. But I had nothing to teach, nobody to listen.

We came to the village road, tree-lined and quiet. Saw the first soul of the morning, an old lady shuffling slowly to Mass. An elder. What could I teach her? That I felt as near to the end of life as she was. Only mine ended in a forest of dreams. I thought even she had her dreams. The dream of the ancients. To live forever in the land called Tír na nÓg. The land where the young Oisín journeyed to, the land of eternal youth. Gold haired, blue eyes, bronzed and brave Oisín. There was a cinema in the next town called the Oisín. The dream screen draped over the small town. Winter nights. Other worlds I glimpsed in imaginings ... an everlasting young summer.

Chapter Eleven

The villagers were beginning to stir. The men shoving Rosary beads in their pockets. The woman tying scarves to their heads while hurrying loitering children along. Another Sunday morning. No word had been spoken. The trap pulled in by the one hotel in the village, just below the church. Jacko got down first and tied the pony to the side railing of the hotel. Axme, Johnny and I climbed down separately. The eyes of the village took us all in: the two tinker men, the tinker boy and me. And I, measured against the tinkers, brought long looks from their eyes. I wanted to run to my own but their clean faces were strange. Wanted to run from the three tinkers but my bond with Johnny held me. In the end I stood by the gate of the church snared between two worlds.

Inside, the church was dark, the candles unlit. The lamp before the Real Presence shone as always; Christ's eternal star. People were still shuffling silently in; the children to the front, the women on one side, the men to the back. I followed Jacko and Axme, keeping in step with Johnny. Dipping my finger in the font, blessing myself, genuflecting, kneeling. "Reserved for men," I read the sign on the outside of the seat. Hoped I wouldn't be noticed in the gloom.

The altar boy came out of the sacristy, holding the candle lighter on high. I couldn't pray in my mind so I watched the boy. His fair fringe made a halo on his forehead as he kindled the six candles. He had trouble with the last one. Three times he tried and I felt sorry for him. On the fourth attempt the flame flickered and he turned, his cheeks red with effort and shame.

The loud bell called the church to rise. I didn't stand on the kneeler as I would at home. I listened to the Latin murmur. Said the responses that I knew. The Kyrie. That was a Greek word. Thought I didn't know much Latin; decided I was better at Greek and smiled with my mind to myself. None of us had a missal where we could read the English for the Latin. Axme carried an ol' black Rosary beads. He was passing his fingers through one of the five mysteries and, judging by his face, I thought it must be the sorrowful ones. Jacko was just silent, praying without words, Latin or English. Johnny had his hands joined, his lips moving, his face intense. I didn't take much notice of the church, only noticed it was very small. The middle aisle was about the same width as the side aisles at home. Even the Christ on the Cross was diminished.

I sat up for the sermon. It was about the lost sheep. It took the priest a long time to find him. Johnny threw me a look that said "he's on about you." Lost. But no shepherd travelled the hills to bring me home. Only turned back, hunted like a sheep that took a by-road. All in an April evening. Like the poem. April. The month of misty evenings. The drover herding the flocks from the darkening pastures. The breaths of the sheep forming a white cloud to lighten the coming night. The lambs, skittish all day, now ran close to the ewes. Calmed by the quiet of evening. The words formed out of the image in my mind:

> "All in an April evening,
> April airs were abroad,
> The sheep with their little lambs,
> Passed me by on the road,
> The sheep with their little lambs,
> Passed my by on the road,
> And I thought on the Lamb of God."

At Carhan bridge I saw the flock, by the still waters of the river.

The sermon ended while I prayed, because the poem was a prayer. The Agnus Dei followed the Consecration. Agnus Dei: Lamb of God. I said it in Latin and pictured the lamb of evening. God was like that I thought. Like evening: peaceful and lonely. The last gospel was said and the priest turned to bless.

He had his hand up to make the sign of the cross but no words carried the cross. I was still wondering at the images in my mind when a voice whispered, too loud for the church. "That's him. The tinkers have him between them." I glanced over my shoulder at the blue uniform. I felt Jacko tense, saw Axme flinch and Johnny, Johnny looked hard at me. The sergeant, like a little boy on tiptoes, looking over Guard Moran's massive shoulder.

Stepping into the centre aisle, he held up his hand to get the priest's attention, as if he was directing traffic. The priest shouting "what's the meaning of this outrage?" The sergeant was spluttering and red-faced as the congregation turned round. I not knowing what to do, whether to run or rest. Jacko and Axme staring straight ahead, their faces closed. Johnny, Johnny moving away from me on his knees.

Above the commotion the sergeant tried to explain, pointing to me, using works like "kidnapped" and "under arrest". Arrest me for what, I thought. Running away from home. Dickens's days. Coming straight up the aisle, Guard Moran reached into the pew to clasp my shoulder. I was pulled off my feet.

"You're coming back home with us, my bright boy," was all he said.

I held back against the pressure of his hand and he jerked me up on my toes. I could smell his uniform, smoke and serge. I heard Johnny shout "let him be" and I found myself pulled like a ragdoll between the great frame of Moran and the tiny fury of Johnny. In the ructions that followed I was nearly pulled asunder, my arms stretched. Another Guard I hadn't noticed joined in, trying to break Johnny's grip. Then Axme caught hold of him and in the end Jacko was stirred. Back and forth like a children's game, the seat used as a lever was forced out of place. People had risen to crane their necks for a better view. I was still in the vice of Moran's hand but Johnny had been prised loose.

The priest came all the way down from the altar, his red round face trembling with rage. When his presence was felt the pulling and hauling stopped. Nobody moved in the sudden silence. Under the arm of Moran I peeped out to see Axme arrested by the other Guard and Jacko being linked by the sergeant. Johnny was free and I thought he was steeped in luck.

"I, ah," the priest cleared his throat and the "I" echoed from the deep stone of the church. In the echo of his hesitance, Jacko moved, knocking the arm that held him and pulling Axme free. Johnny was already at the door and I felt the cold air on my legs. The door closed, swinging back and forth. Jacko turned, before the congregation, back to the door. His blue eyes looked at me for what seemed a long time, blue ice breaking over my burning face. No word of blame could say more and I had no answer. I tried to open my mouth but it was dry. No word ready and even so too late. The door closed in my face. Nobody moved.

The sergeant and the priest spoke together, in whispers. The priest looked satisfied and addressed the congregation. "My brethren, would you kindly face the altar and we'll finish the Mass.'

He glanced at me once before walking slowly up the aisle. People can hurt with their eyes, I thought. I'd rather have the strap then the cold kill. The Mass continued but I didn't heed it. It ended when Jacko shut the door. Like leaving the confession box without absolution. The sergeant didn't wait for the prayers after Mass. He took me by the shoulder and gave a short nod to the door. I looked at him and through him before getting up. The Guards slipped out on the tips of their boots, scraping the tiles

Chapter Twelve

The sun had swept the village clean and bright while we were at Mass. The light dazzled my eyes and for a while I couldn't see. Didn't want to see because the light had dimmed my life. There was no sign of the trap. The railings of the Towers hotel were like prison bars. They had escaped and in their freedom imprisoned me with a penance I could never pay. I walked with my head down between the Sergeant and Guard Moran, their blue legs moving as one. I pretended I was cutting off the rest of their bodies. The squad car was parked in the street, big, black and shining with importance. They put me in the back seat, behind the Sergeant. The guard I didn't know sat in with me. He was young and red-faced and awkward when he spoke, which was only in single words. Guard Moran started the car and it coughed dead instantly. "Give it choke, Guard," the Sergeant told him.

I wondered did he address all the guards like that? Like having everybody called the same name. A common world; the world of the Father, the Brother and the Guard. The black trinity. Blue too. Black and blue like the colour of hurt. The car started the second time, then stalled and Guard Moran said "choke, is it, the devil choke it." They all laughed. The third time it started and faced home. Seventeen miles and the questions began. Long miles of earnest anger because not one word did I utter. All the questions got into my mind. Made me blush, touched my temper, hammered at my head but could not break my iron silence. They made me look at them. Their country faces looking flushed. Holding my eyes, eyes that saw but refused to recognise. I was amazed at the smallness of them. Their uniforms that made me jump when I was cycling home late of a winter's evening now held no fear for me. In the end the Sergeant threatened me with jail and I wanted to laugh in his face because only the judge who came monthly to the courthouse had that power. Power, that's what gave strength to my silence. The power I felt by the camp fire. The strong thread of the dream that was still holding me in the clearing of day. The night the season of my solitude began, took on a meaning beyond words. And no word did they gain. The road swept by; the seventeen miles of silence, of Sunday.

Soon we were at the viaduct and I watched the sun fade and find the hills again and again, like waves of light. Shadow and shine on the reaches of my mind. Nearly home and never home. I felt something pull me two ways something I didn't understand. I thought of my parents. Flinching at the clip round the ear I would surely get. The early to bed for a week. No half-crown pocket money. Patches. The gabble of questions. Breda finding fault ...

The car turned under the viaduct and we were into the shadow of the hills. Like a dark curtain they were strung round the town. Was it to escape the hill I left? To find out like the boy in the fable, whether what I saw was gold at the foot of a hill or the reflection of an evening sun on a cottage window. I had to touch it to find its truth. And what if it was a reflection, when the sun set it would die? And now I was looking at the world through pale glass. But the evening would return, return in my own reflections.

They had given up on me by now and started talking about football and fishing, turfooting and the weather. Agreeing with the sergeant on every subject. At Kells station Guard Moran said, "there's rain in Dingle." I looked out over the bay and saw the dark squall over Dingle. The guards fell silent after grunting agreement with Moran. The sky was threatening as we drove down to Deelis bridge. Dingle rain spread across to sprinkle the windscreen. Soon all I could see was a steaming blur, the rain hopping off the road. The windscreen wipers couldn't clean the rain fast enough and Guard Moran crouched forward over the steering wheel, his bushy eyebrows pulled down over his peering eyes.

"A fright to God," the Sergeant muttered.

The young Guard answered, "enough to frighten the daylights out of a man too."

"Indeed," the Sergeant said gravely, "it's dark enough, indeed."

Guard Moran gave a little cough and the young guard echoed it by clearing his throat. "Indeed." It just struck me that every time the Sergeant agreed with what was said he uttered, "indeed." I looked sideways at him but he didn't seem to know they were mocking him.

I looked away out the window and pictured four faces peppered by the rain. I wondered were they on their way yet. The pony would be steaming with sweat and water-wet in this weather I thought. I shivered in my mind and for the first time felt my own clothes stick to my back. My face felt dry and dirty. Hunger made my stomach rumble like thunder and I tried to stop the noise by tensing my tummy. I wondered would I have to go to last Mass if I got home on time; put on my Sunday suit, wear my Sunday shoes, the black shiny ones that creaked.

The car took a sharp turn, Guard Moran locking the wheel to the right. Carhan bridge. Almost home. I could follow the rest of the road; up a few furlongs then a wide bend left and a bit of flat to the bottom of the Height. The long Height that my father had to walk up when he was carrying me on the bar. Levelling off at the top all the way to Carhan road. All along the broken footpath people were hurrying to and from Mass. Braving the wild wet wind.

Halfway back to town Guard Moran looked to the sergeant and nodded his head about me.

"We may as well drive him to the door. The mother'll want to know the story," he said as if I wasn't there. I didn't like the way he said "the mother" but didn't let on.

At the cross I looked up the Rock. It looked cold and empty. Beenatee above it was lost in a white mist. I thought of an old woman's face pressed to a window. It seemed so long ago. Yesterday. A long time ago. Like a story from *Our Boys*, only I was the tale. Maybe a part of my own life was just a story. A dream of yesterday. A time of forests and freedom. Mountains and meadow. The journey of my life. From the dawn of the morning star to the dusk on the window of evening. A reflection of a lonely God. Me and an old woman's face. A fierce urge to see her seized me but the car had already turned right. Her world and mine partitioned by pride. Her loneliness framed in a broken window, mine mirrored in a broken dream. The old graveyard. The corner at Bawnies Field. I was home.

My mother came to the door, the *Sunday Press* in her hand. I was ready for ructions. The Sergeant got out with me, holding his cap to his head as he hurried to the shelter of the hall. I walked behind him and looked up to my mother's face for a sign.

"Why didn't you take your coat along with you lad?" she said as if I'd only been up town.

I was too surprised to answer for a second and finally said "I forgot."

The Sergeant and my mother laughed out loud as if I cracked the biggest joke in the world. "Go on in and have a shin-heat for yourself," she ruffled my hair.

I blessed myself with a drop from the holy water font and entered the kitchen. Breda was washing the breakfast ware in the scullery and she stuck her head round the door. "My, oh my, the wild rover has returned."

I didn't answer back and knew I won her silence. I went to the range and let down the guard to free the heat. Taking the poker I pushed it through the five holes to stir the fire. Sparks flew out and I warmed my hands. I sat down on the armchair. I looked round the kitchen. It felt strange. I thought of an expression of my father's; "out of place." Myths had made away with me, locking me in a prison past. And now I was afraid to come out of time. The kitchen door burst open and Patches ran in. He stopped instantly, in midstride, when he saw me. Without saying "hello," he whispered with a look to the door. "The bleddy guards are at the front."

"They're not bleddy, they're blue," I corrected him.

"Ah, bleddy" … he said.

He crept Indian-like to the window and peered out through the constant rain.

The squad car revved up and voices were raised in goodbye.

The front door closed. Patches stayed silent at the window. Breda dried the ware in the scullery. I heard my mother's step on the stairs. I sat and closed my mind to all but the fading sound of the squad car.

It was done. I was home. The clock struck twelve. The Angelus. The call. I didn't answer now. My world of ten ended as the last chime lingered into silence. The rain ... Only the rain was constant.

Part II

"Now I possess ... something else, called soul. I am told that the soul never dies, is always searching and searching.
... Instead of succumbing to my homesickness, I have told myself that my home is everywhere."

Vincent Van Gogh

Chapter Thirteen

Summer came. The world was new. I passed into fifth class. Warm days: blue mornings and the glint of gold on the evening hill. Playing with time from June to September. Work in the black bog. Pestering my father to take me to the creamery. Milking the quiet cow and spraying the hot milk into the roof of my mouth. Running through the creamery fields with Carlow. Taking Patches to Bosses Strand to crab fish among the rocks. Wandering along the dunes, watching the waves break along the jagged shoreline. Playing football in the Avenue after tea. Sword fighting with skinned branches in the Big Terret. Crossing the pier road to the small Terret to see the trains shunting. In a short time the station would close down for good. The railway men would leave for Tralee and Cork. The six o'clock evenings would fall silent, the station to ruin. On the longest day roaming far and wide collecting for the bonfire. Dragging branches that the older boys cut in the old graveyard. The boys from the Rock coming down the Marian showing off their tractor tyres. The blackest smoke always came from the Rock but the Marian had the biggest fire. The longest night, with dancing on the concrete square under the ESB light. People from the country in gawking at the fire. The smell of carbon as the tops of Golden Syrup tins blew off. The whooping children, losing their mothers to the excitement of the night.

I ran with Patches all night, minding him. Letting him throw a small branch on the fire. Cheering with the rest when the flames leapt into the dark summer night. I was reckoned in every hunt … "ink ank under the bank, ink ank out." Out. Like the fire at dawn with only a cluster of Secondary school boys smoking by it's ashes. Grey. The morning when the summer began to die. Only a smouldering in a dark circle. I always felt sad that morning as if something had died on me.

In July I turned the green sop of hay. My father gave a widow woman a couple of days. After the turning had dried I made the cocks of hay. My father called them wynds. It was cold in the morning, but when the sun stood over my head I had to take my jumper off. At one o'clock each day the woman brought a basket of food; tea and sandwiches and a cut of Gateaux cake. I loved eating in the open, lying against the warmed hay. I worked right into the evening, and when at last I went home my mother had to rub calamine lotion on my arms and neck. The sunburn peeled in a day and I had my undercoat for the hottest sun. I got a half-crown a day from the woman. I felt rich after the four days had seen the hay saved.

August. The month of visitors. The pale English cousins arriving. Two boys who couldn't play football. Wouldn't climb the hills. Thought bullocks were cows. Even Breda was better than them. Every time I said anything to them they answered "eh." I kept ducking away from them. I was played out from running, after three weeks. My mother warned me to go to the station to see them off. That was my fastest run! Anything to see the back of them. I liked the railway station; with people and excitement coming and going. Coming in tears, and going in tears. Different though. This would be the last summer for the railway into town. The line would end at Killarney. My father said it was emigration that made them cry. The train made a sad sound going over the black bridge before it went out of view. Only the puffing smoke rising in the distance told me where it was. Gone. Journeys to remind me.

September. Everything ended and began. Back to school. Summer a memory, and always the glint of gold on an evening hill. "The boys' Primary school will re-open on Tuesday!" The announcement from the pulpit sunk into my stomach. One day. The leaves would fall. The rains gather on the hills. The curtain would be drawn at tea-time. The evening would shadow my soul, catching my sadness. September. It would come again because the seasons turned, and when the full circle passed I was in the primary year. English, Irish and arithmetic. I learned history and geography too but they were not included in the exam. The Brother kept reminding the class of the importance of the Primary Cert. At Christmas he said time was running out. By Easter he was telling us to pull our socks up. He gave the class two compositions a week; English on Tuesday and Irish on Thursday, with sums in between. If a comp was badly written, the Brother would read it out loud and make fun of the boy. I didn't like comps about "a day in the life of." I felt it was silly writing about a day in the life of a boot or a coat.

At noon we had Christian Doctrine. The Canon came in to ask questions from the catechism. He had something in his throat and took out his white hanky to spit phlegm into it. He laughed with the Brother, a funny laugh through his teeth. His cold black figure frightened me. He asked me who baptised Our Lord. I couldn't think and tried, "Moses" but realised I had the wrong testament by the way he glared over his glasses. Whenever a boy saw him approaching in the street he'd run down the nearest side-street. The Brother brought it up one day. "Why do some of you boys run from the Canon?" The class shifted unreasily, but no one owned up. "Show a little respect in future," he ordered. When we passed the priests, we were to salute, like soldiers. If we had caps on we were to raise them.

The nearer the exam came the harder the Brother became. His face, neck and bald head reddened like a turkey-cock. He kept anyone who didn't do their homework inside after school. The dole man's son was his pet and he minded the class while the Brother was out. He called him by his first name along with any other boy whose father had clean hands.

In May I picked bluebells and water lillies for the school altar. The boys who had gardens brought roses and other flowers. A boy from the country brought piss-a-beds, thinking they were buttercups. On May Day I picked May Flower and went around sticking it thro' letter boxes. It wasn't a flower really but a soft green branch. I didn't know why it was put through letter boxes at all. My father said it was tradition. My mother said, "we've enough to do besides clearing up tradition from the hall."

I went to the May devotions each evening at half-seven. The May altar was piled with primroses; bluebells genuflected in tall vases. Our Lady was called Queen of the May in one hymn. I tried to sit in the middle aisle. Sometimes she was on the outside of the pew, opposite me, her hands joined by a rosary, covering her pale cheek. An Aran bonnet on her fair head slanted over her left eye. Sometimes she looked across and I pretended not to see. Then I would sneak a glance and she'd be looking piously to the altar. When Benediction was over we genuflected together and turned down the aisle with her in front. One evening towards the end of May our elbows touched and she smiled "sorry" to me. I smiled silently back, my cheeks glowing. Out in the evening air I had a feeling of happiness that lifted my eyes to the sky. It was like coming out of confession, cleansed and forgiven.

I lost her in the crowded back porch and ran all the way home. The weight of two years lifted and my heart beat freely again. After that evening I'd cycle up after her whenever she went up town for a message. Smile, and turn at the cross when she wasn't looking and back home again. Whenever I saw her I thought of Johnny. I hadn't been with him for over two years and I only said hello to him now. I felt he wanted to stop and I did too, but there was a distance between us.

Two weeks before the Primary an Inspector Brother came to the school. We were lined up around the classroom and warned to behave. A smiling, fresh-faced Brother entered. He never stopped smiling, as if it was painted to his face. He asked a few questions in Irish first, in the presence of the teacher. Then he said, "All right now Brother," and the teacher went out, closing the door behind him.

The Inspector asked simple questions like, "How many persons in the One God?" He'd push up close to the boy he'd asked and put his hand on his thigh. Smiling all the while, his hand crept up the boy's leg as he coaxed, "What's the answer to that now?" The whole class was laughing and the boy he was questioning made them laugh more by going, "oh, oh!" to the smiling hand. I wished I had long trousers like some of the boys. He passed them by without a touch. When he came, I was ready. His hand was on my knee while he was asking, "Name the sixth Commandment." His soft clammy hand climbed as I was thinking, his fingers going under my trousers and pulling the elastic of my underpants. I stepped back and his hand fell out. Thinking quickly I said, "Thou shalt not commit adultery!" I said, "thou" strongly at him and his face lost its smile for an instant. He passed on and slowly shuffled round the class. Everybody thought he was a great gas when he left.

The Primary Friday fell in the middle of June. I'd gone to bed early the night before without opening a book. I didn't have to be at school until ten and I moped around after breakfast. Constantly to the window to see if anyone was going up. I finally left with my ruler, pencil, rubber and nib. It felt strange without my schoolbag, as I walked in the early sunshine. I met the Sergeant's son at the Church gates and he showed me the formula for compound interest he'd written on his arm.

The class was in the playground; nobody was running. Small groups of boys stood against the wide walls; each with a ruler, pencil, rubber and nib. No bell rang out but the Brother clapped his hand to beckon us in. Filing silently by him, on our own now. The room looked different but I couldn't think why for a minute. The desks had been pulled apart leaving a good space between each to stop copying. The class was told to pick a desk and I chose the second last one on the fifth class side of the room. The Secondary Superior was to watch the class. He told us to read the instructions carefully. Mentioned the time allowed for each subject and above all, that there was to be no cogging. He looked at his watch and said, "Start now!"

The Irish comp was easy and I wrote four and a half pages of foolscap. There was a break of ten minutes and the English paper was next. "A day in the life of ..."

I went home for dinner, pleased with my writing. My father said, "How did the scholar do?" and I said, "Dead simple." The next subject was arithmetic and I worried on the way back, especially about the combined fraction. It cancelled fairly well, one seventh was my answer. If it was one quarter or a half, even an eighth I'd know everything was alright but one seventh? It looked awkward, wrong, and I went over it again when I'd finished the paper. The answer was the same. I dropped my pen and listened to the other nibs scratching away. "Time's up!"

The Superior looked up from his wrist and I shifted in my seat.

Outside, the Brother had the answers and I asked about the fraction. "One seventh!" he said, "Have a good holiday, you deserve it." The class broke up in excited chants:

"No more Latin,
No more French,
No more sitting
on a hard old bench.

No more Irish,
No more Bans
No more English,
No more Tans."

The English were the cause of the five young boys being blown to smithereens near the old workhouse. I saw the grim grey cross sanctifying the soil where the bits of boys were scattered. It was said that the man who owned the field couldn't graze his horses in it afterwards. The animals went mad with the smell of blood on the spring grass. That was the war of brothers; the field they fought over lies unredeemed. Every Easter a band left the Fair Field to march Over the Water to the graveyard. It was called after them in Irish. Keelavarnogue: "Rest of young men." A decade of the Rosary was recited at the Republican plot. A long grave with a scatter of white gravel covering. A wreath was laid every year. "The flowers withered but their memory would never grow old!" A man with staring eyes and white hair dropped his voice to a whisper last Easter when making the speech. It was like the few seconds silence between thunder and lightening and I remembered it after I'd forgotten his face, a stranger. White hair ... white gravel and the white cross at the side of a lonely road. History. I'd be learning that next year I thought, as the chants faded outside the schoolgates.

Chapter Fourteen

The summer passed in long days at the White Strand. Cycling there on my big sister's bike with Buster Brown. He was my constant companion all summer. Whether picking blackberries in a jam-jar or hunting for wild goats on the hills above Coonana. Holding running races round the ring. The big boys measured out a mile, taking a tape twenty four and a half times round. Some evenings they were still running and it dark. The magic miler was Ronnie Delaney, gilded in the gold of evening. I could hear the pounding feet when I was called for the Rosary. My father knelt up on the sofa. "The Lord will open my lips, and my tongue shall announce his praise!" My big sister finished work at half-seven and came in near the end. She never bowed the knee. I thought maybe working in the convent all day made her holy enough.

Buster Brown was in the Secondary but I palled up with him after swopping comics. He had a white plastic football with WEMBLEY written on it. He said it was a soccer ball and when I said I couldn't soc he laughed his head off. The Secondary boys were playing soccer in secret over in the Avenue. It was wrong to play it and the Superior was bucking when he found out. I watched Buster play in the evenings. I was the scout in case a teacher came by and saw them soccering the ball.

I played in a street league that summer in Gaelic football. I was made captain when I scored with my left leg in the first game. If I kicked it with my right nobody took any care. It was Buster who made me practise with my left.

In the final the Rock played the Marian. We were favourites but the Rock scored a goal before we knew where we were. The Marian fought back to take the lead by two points. Time was running out when Johnny came on as sub. He fielded a great ball in midfield and went off on a solo run, selling dummies by the new time. I was playing full-back and crouched to tackle him. Something wild and free about his flying legs mesmerised me. An image of a red deer in flight across a mountain, across my mind. A fraction, maybe one-seventh of a second, mistimed and I missed him. His shot hammered the back of the net with all his power. His eyes were bright, his red hair flying like a flag in the slight breeze, his cheeks flushed in victory as he walked back. I passed him in my disappointment and he said, "It's a draw now, little treasure." I turned to say, "But you're a point in the lead," when I understood his meaning and said instead, "great equalizer Johnny." I took the kick out and the final whistle went. The winners got a set of medals and the captain a cup.

The endless summer went on and long into September. Kerry won the All-Ireland and the bonfires blazed. Kerry was called the Kingdom and the subject hills rose red into the summer sky the night the team brought home the cup.

The Races brought the last bit of excitement to the town. I took Patches out to the course and he won a china dog at a raffle stall. There were only three horses in some races. A man with a loud-hailer shouted, "clear the course" before every race. Patches took it upon himself to do the man's job, shouting at the top of his voice. I pretended I wasn't with him.

Mary had a stall of apples and biscuits, sweets and minerals. I bought everything there because she was Mary. There was a man with a monkey on his shoulder wandering around trying to get people to do the three-card trick. I kept going to the paddock to admire my favourite horse. He was called Starfleet and he was the colour of a silken night. A white star arrowed his proud forehead. He won the last race, the Cahirciveen Plate, and I went home happy.

After tea I ducked off without Patches to the Fair Field. The street was still crowded, the pub door not getting a chance to close. I heard the music from the fun-fair and could make out the words when I got to the Secondary school. "Teenager in Love" played softly to the evening and in the words I felt a new loneliness. I wandered around under the chair-o-planes, the seesaws. Under the happy laughter of the boys and girls, under the heel of the evening.

I saw her later on as the hill fell under the shadow of night. Standing by the roulette table, a fistful of pennies lost on the whirling wheel. My eyes had come down from the hill to alight on her bowed head. Her sister by her side, but something told me she was alone. I walked quietly over and stood on the other side of a countryman who was by her side. The wheel was spun and I pulled a quick penny from my pocket. I placed it on the black. She was on the blue and the man was red. The black paid and I took the penny along with my own. She looked over and I caught her eyes. The light was soft on her face when she smiled and my stomach turned over. I forced a slow shy smile in return and "Teenager in Love" played again. After a spell the man left and we were side by side. The fair lights reflected the hidden gold in her hair. She wore a red pleated skirt with a white polo jumper. Her pale face was touched with colour.

We played on, exchanging silent smiles if either of us won. She had a way of lifting her narrow shoulders and letting them drop when she lost. I wanted her to win more than myself, to win and stay by my side. She kept playing on the blue and reds, losing more often than not. I knew the black was the better ratio. She was one age with me so she must have done ratios in school. The night wore on and her pennies ran out. She turned to her sister and sent her home. I felt more alone with her than ever.

The people were scattering for the dance. The records stopped playing. It was late and turning cold. She had one penny left and played the red. I didn't care so I played the blue. The black paid again. I had four pennies left and wanted to share them with her. Wanted to share the night, the lonely walk home ... "Try these," I spoke and my voice sounded strange. Her hands were on the side of the table and she pushed them away. Her eyes widened; she was ready for flight.

"I couldn't," her voice was small, her shoulders dropped as if she'd lost.

"It's only tuppence," I pursued in an indifferent way. She held out her hand and I passed the two pennies without touching her.

"Thanks, I must pay you back," she insisted.

"If you want to," I answered and played the black. She lost after two spins and waited while I played my last penny. It was blue. I looked at her and she let her shoulders drop for me.

I smiled and she said, "I'm afraid to go home alone." Her head lowered, her face was framed in the shadow of her tumbling hair. I wanted to lift her chin, to look in the sad eyes and tell her "it's alright."

I spoke over her head, "I'm going straight home, you can come with me." Together we walked away from the fair, an awkward silence stumbling along with us. She spoke first, asking how I did in the Primary. We talked about the Primary as I conveyed her through the crowded street. Couples were walking up the Iveragh ballroom steps, arm in arm. The music deafening at the door opened. I could still hear high notes at the cross. She asked me "would you like to be old enough to go dancing?" and I said "no." Her quick silence disagreed with me. Her shoulder brushed mine as we passed the old graveyard. That's what she was afraid of! She stayed very close until we came to the corner at Bawnies Field. We parted under the ESB pole in the square. She said she'd pay me back on Sunday. I wondered why I didn't feel lonely when I said goodbye to her.

My mother went to first Mass Sunday and I asked her was the announcement made. It was. I heard it again at second Mass and the thought of going upstairs stayed with me all day. She was at second Mass; I saw her receiving. She wore a black mantilla on her head which set off her hair, like a sombre sunset.

There was a match in the field after dinner. I didn't go back until quarter to four because it was due to start at three-thirty. Buster said the GAA were always behind the times. He called it the grab all association. He had to pay to go in but I got in for nothing.

She came down the sideline during half-time and held out tuppence. I took it quickly for fear anyone might see. I had met the Sergeant's son below and was watching the match with him. He smoked on the quiet, buying one or two Afton at a time. A shop down Railway Street sold them loose. He was always asking for a butt; a hard case. "Who is the little peach?" he asked when she walked away, blushing.

I just answered, "She's from the Marian" and he said, "I didn't know you had any bit budding down there."

He was talking about the two dots showing through the white blouse. I went red but the second half started and he didn't notice. One of the Secondary teachers was playing in midfield for the town. He was the hardest teacher, the Sergeant's son told me. He hadn't a very good catch, missing the ball every time he jumped. He wore a hair-net and the crowd were laughing at him. Only old women had hair-nets and he looked like an overgrown nancy boy. He was from the North. Mick O'Connell soared into the blue sky, a majestic man in red. He was from Valentia.

I called for Buster after the match. "Will Buster be out?" I asked his sister.

"No! he'll be in." She made fun and went to get him. She was a cheeky squirt. We discussed the match. Buster never talked; he discussed! He was selling some second-hand books and I bought a first year Longmans Latin for one and six pence and a European History in Irish for a shilling. His father was sitting by the kitchen window reading the *Sunday Independent* and spoke to me, "God help us! European history in Irish, and I suppose them buckos can teach you to saw wood in Irish too?"

I laughed at his tone and said, "they'd have a job." He was a carpenter. I went home for tea and put my new books in my satchel. I could smell the musty leather and I was back in the classroom again.

The evening passed, restlessly. No magic mile outside my window. No kick-up in the square. No ink, no ank. No hunt. No wild tomorrow. Only two girls skipping by the ESB pole, one end of the rope tied to the pole with one of the girls turning. The skipping girl was shouting, "pepper" and the rope was twisted fast and hard. When it was twisted slowly it was called "salt." The girl twisting was chanting "All she wants is gold and silver, all she wants is a nice young man." I was leaning on the window-sill in the kitchen, staring out. My mother came over to

95

have a peep and said, "She'd badly want a man," and I blushed. It was the other girl's turn and my heart skipped. The girl twisting was calling the alphabet, ABC and trapped her on my initials. My mother was going out for a walk. I hoped they'd finish before she got her scarf on. I was blushing but pleased at the same time. She was caught on L next and then her own initials.

"All the boys are fighting for her." I thought of the narrow look the Sergeant's son gave her budding body. "She loves him the best." That was me and I wondered how the other girl knew. She must have seen the two of us together the night of the races. The strange night, the roulette with loneliness. I felt it now, again, for no reason except seeing her in a childlike game. A child when she skips and grown up when afraid to go home alone. I too was growing when I felt alone in a hunt, in a children's game. Was she thinking of me now when my name was shouted to the night? Did she feel the darkness come down as I did? Bringing my name to her lips as my lips uttered hers, under my breath. "Anna!" In darkness and in silence and in love.

The light came on the ESB pole and they gathered up the game. Anna's friend went up town and she skipped off into the night. I was alone. My mother had gone. My father had strolled up town long before. Breda and Patches were upstairs and my big sister was at the pictures. I turned to the glow of the fire. Closing the window at the top, drawing the curtain. I crossed to the armchair by the fire and sat down. It was dark in the kitchen and the fire was cosy. Closing my eyes, I let the warmth seep into my body. I curled up on the chair, one hand on my thigh. I thought about Anna and her body shaped before my mind. My hand brushed against her, against my thigh. It hollowed my stomach and my mouth felt dry. My hand rubbed up my thigh between my legs. I pulled it away quickly. A pain. A pain and a pleasure. My hand found its way back, feeling, rubbing. I felt a hard throbbing and I frightened her presence from my mind.

The results came out in a soft September morning. I was upstairs with the big boys. Learning to call arithmetic "maths." I learned my first Latin noun, *mensa*, which meant table. The

96

vocative, "O table!" a noble language. "O noble table!" The Primary world had faded; I was crossing the Alps with Hannibal. The first year was called down to get the results. A boy from the country came first, the doleman's son was second. I was third.

I saw Anna after the Rosary that evening. The nights were drawing in but it was still light at eight. She was coming out of Dan's with a packet of chewing gum in her hand, offering me some and saying "congrats" on the Primary. I was pleased because she said it in a grown-up way. I thanked her twice. I enquired about her results and she said she passed too. She showed me a picture of a film star that was wrapped round the gum. She said she'd love to be a film star. I looked at the picture. Sophia Loren. "Isn't she gorgeous?" she asked arching her eyebrows, looking for more that the answer to a picture. I blushed for no reason and her lips half smiled.

"She'll do," I said shortly. She pushed out her lower lip, pouting. I felt sorry for the way I spoke and offered to collect the film stars for her. I didn't often chew gum.

She said, "would you, would you really?" and her mouth opened in a warm smile.

I answered "I will, I will really."

She slapped my arm saying "Oh you" and we were both laughing and happy together. We talked for some time under the ESB pole until her sister cycled over, calling her. "You're wanted home." She was startled and looked to her house. Her mother was standing by the gate looking across hard.

"My mother! I must go. So long," and she was gone, running.

Autumn. The brown season rushed away in the winter winds. The trees lost their coats. The tide rose high on the Fertha. The ditches were swollen with rains. The hills huddled, flattened by wind and rain and my eyes could see clearly no more. First I thought it was the shine on the blackboard. I was sitting with the Sergeant's son and I started asking him a word here and there. I told Brother Main there was a shine on the board and he angled it back a bit. We had him for English and he kept harping on Romantic Ireland; "dead and gone, it's with

97

O'Leary in the grave!" I looked up the hill from the classroom window... grey grass under a wild sky. Brother Main was easy and interesting. He brought *Treasure Island* to Cahirciveen: smugglers coming ashore at Kells Strand and drinking rum in Cáitín Baiters. "Use your imaginations," he implored. "Dream, dream, dream. The mountains, the valley and the sea. You boys don't know how lucky you are with the Trinity of nature around here. Do you know there are boys in London and New York who wake to mountains of cold concrete. Aren't their mornings hard?" he asked and the class burst out laughing.

Maths were the worst, taking down the figures from the blackboard. Sometimes I squinted and got by. To Christmas, grey frost on the ground, hardening the grass. The town coming to life, the Christmas tree on the street outside the dance hall. The shops decorated with red berries and snips of tinsel. Christmas holidays, secret soccer in the Avenue. I loved playing, trapping and dribbling the ball and heading a cross to the net. It made me feel above the Gaelic crowd. There were some boys who wouldn't kick the ball along the ground, it was a foreign act. English. I liked being different. All through the holidays I played, using my father's old shoes. They were caked in mud when the day softened.

Chapter Fifteen

A black frost fell early Christmas Eve. It was gone when I got up. My father had to brave it in the dark morning. The cold held solid all day. I went to confession after tea. It was the last night out in the carols. I was out singing the three nights before Christmas. My voice hadn't broken yet though I was thirteen. Mr Morley led the whole choir, boys and girls. The nuns weren't allowed in the world. I sang best when we came to the Marian, under the ESB pole. Beneath Beenatee, facing home. My door opening and my mother leaning in the shadows, Patches by her side. "Silent Night" my favourite carol ascended into the cold and crowded night sky.

I was singing at Midnight Mass and had to be up in the choir at half-eleven. The Church was empty, nobody keeping vigil before the crib. I prayed to the Eternal Infant in the silence. A peace I didn't know was in me descended. I looked over to the girls' choir. Anna was in the front row. She felt my eyes and glanced across. She smiled, a faraway smile, and took me with her. I smiled slowly back and a warm rush coloured my cheeks. I wanted to reach across and touch her hand but I only withdrew my smile and turned my eyes to the crib.

The Church was filling and the organ began to play "Adeste Fideles." The sacred sadness of the Latin carol reached out in the Church: "venite, venite in Bethlehem." Into my village by the side of a hill, stretching white with drifts of silence to the cold sky. The hill farmers keeping watch over their sheep, out with lantern and collie. "Dream, dream, dream," and I built Bethlehem in a night, on the side of Beenatee. Mass started and the choir was on its feet. I felt happy; somewhere deep within, the silent night rested. A new peace, a growing peace, settled over me. I would cherish that night when other nights blew black and bitter. We all filed down the stairs to communion. The white host was cool on my tongue. I walked slowly out the tower door and up the stairs to the choir, alone but for the body of Christ. I closed my eyes and said the prayers after communion in my mind. Three priests were giving out communion; I watched the three aisles of people shuffling slowly to the altar rails, hungry for the bread of life.

I was sad when the last blessing was made. It was over. I went out into the iced air. The snow had stopped falling. On the street the first coat lay, stretching evenly down. I walked quietly home with Buster, my shoes crunching deep prints in the snow. Boys were skating down the middle of the street shouting and throwing snowballs. Buster wasn't talking much and I was glad. I wished him a Happy Christmas at my door. He said, "and the same to you Buster." That's why he was called the name. I had a feed of sausages and bacon and it was going for two before I went to bed.

It was Christmas day then. A light fall of snow fell Christmas morning and I was happy just to watch the world turn white. The fire was warm in the range; my mother had been baking Christmas cake. A rich currant cake and a golden brown madeira. Everything smelled sweet and warm, pure and white. Christmas day.

I took Patches for a walk to the Obs after breakfast. The cold, clean air helped to sharpen an appetite for the turkey. I read the plaque on the gate for Patches. "Meteorological Observatory." I told him it was for telling the weather. He thought it was foolish. I liked to watch the giant balloon go up; they released one every day. It was said if you found where it landed you'd get ten shillings. I never heard tell of anyone claiming it.

We turned for home, facing Knocknadobar. The snow had stopped falling. A sprinkle of white settled on the highest peak. My shoes crunched deep prints in the ground. Boys were skating down the middle of the street, mindful of the odd car. I smelled the roast turkey in the hall when I returned. It made my mouth water.

My father drove in on the Creamery tractor. Even on Christmas day he had to work. I went to meet him at the door asking if I could go out with him. He usually said "no" first, but today he said, "get your wellingtons." The table was set for six, my mother and two sisters busy at the range. I showed my father my new pullover. Patches had a new pair of trousers and Breda got her first pair of nylons. She paraded up and down the kitchen for my father. Her seams were crooked and I joked to Patches about it. She looked awkward, a child dressed up as a woman. My big sister had a new pair of high heels; she called them stiletto. It sounded like Italian scissors. Dangerous! My father had one leg of turkey and I had the other one. I ate it without a fork and cleaned my plate. I had trifle and my father's fresh cream for dessert. I got up first, full to the brim.

My mother said she'd keep the Turkish delight from the box of Black Magic chocolates. The wind whipped my cheeks for the three miles to the Creamery. There wasn't a living soul on the road. The fields stretched cold and the green was gone with shadow. All around, from the hill to the edge of the river, the colour was approaching night.

I warmed up helping my father feed the cattle with bales of hay. They ate it sheltering against a bare ditch. The cows were inside, tied to their stalls. The milkers were fed first to coax the warm white spray from them. I liked to smell the cowhouse, the hay and milk mingling.

By five o'clock they were bedded down for the night. I stood alone in the dark yard while my father locked the doors. He left the tractor in the yard and wheeled his bike from the wall of the cowhouse. He turned his flashlamp on and I jumped up on the bar. It was hard going, pedalling uphill for the first two miles. The night wind was cutting and my wellington slipped loose, but I was happy my father wasn't alone on Christmas Day.

The town was empty, not a shop was open. My father said, "The Deserted Village, by Oliver Goldsmith," in a solemn voice and I laughed because that was all he recited. We both pushed up to the fire when we got in. The girls and Patches were having their tea. Plates of Mikado biscuits, Custard Creams, Kimberley, madeira cake, Christmas pudding and barm brack.

The red candle in the middle of the table. Round shadows

101

from the balloons on the tree. The decorations dimming the light as they triangled across the ceiling. The kettle singing on the range. Cold turkey for my tea. Christmas night.

My father drinking a bottle of stout and I turning up my nose when he offered it. Breda with red lemonade and Patches the big bottle of lemon soda. I had a bottle of wonder orange and my mother and big sister sipped sherry. The chocolates passed around according to age. My father telling stories of olden times. Laughing at the hard times of his youth. Going back to the places where he left his boyhood. Walking in his bare feet across a slough on a frosty morning to get to school. A square of bread and a bottle of buttermilk to see him through the day. Years.

The long night passed too soon. The sofa was drawn up to the fire. My mother brought in an extra bucket of turf. Breda shrieked with laughter when my big sister produced a packet of Sweet Afton and my mother lit up. She tried to inhale but ended up coughing and red in the face. "Oh, she's in hysterics again," she laughed with Breda. My father had another bottle of stout and started to hum, and with Patches saying "Give us a few bars," in a man to man voice, Breda started to giggle again. He sang "Oft in the Stilly Night," his voice young and clear. His mind must have turned back the years. He told us about the sing-songs in his father's house. The all-night wedding dances, breaking up with the dawn. Music and dancing at the crossroads of a summer's evening. I could imagine his fair and lively face in the young season of his life. The evening sun catching the soft blue of his eyes. Only his hair was lost now, lost like his boyhood, forever.

As he talked my mind started to trace my own little life. I was four and it was a wild and wet Christmas Eve. The front door had to be barricaded with chairs. My mother was alone with four small children. Patches was only a baby with red curls. I lay in bed listening to the howling wind. It shook the front of my window in the upper room. A blue Christmas candle stood flickering faintly at the window, showing my father the way. He had to cycle out to the Creamery to see a cow calving. I couldn't sleep and I pretended when my mother looked in. Finally a knock sounded above the wind. He was home. I heard his voice, "Is the little man asleep?" and he opened the door. I said, "Did you follow my light?" and blinked my tired eyes to the candle. He said nothing for a spell, just looked strangely at me. Then he came over and held a brown box out to me. Sitting up in bed I put my arms round his cold neck and he held me whispering "I followed, I followed, but I couldn't find home." He held me tightly, hurt me, and I felt his cheek. It was wet. I said in a whisper to match his, "But my Daddy, you are home," and his voice caught as he said bitterly, "God forgive, God forgive my way. Open the parcel I brought you," he said calmly and he released me. It was a grey horse with a red bridle and a silver key. My father wound him up and the horse was a bucking bronco. It was the only toy I ever owned.

My father was talking about when we were in the country and teasing me. I used to sit on the ditch of the hayfield, imitating the curlew. In the long lonely summer when I was six. The evening darkening over the slough. The fields and the silences stretching endlessly to the distant foothills. Only the sound of the lonesome curlew and my echo, his only answer. My father used to call me, "the curly curlew" and it embarrassed me now.

He got my big sister to sing and she sang, "Wooden Heart." I liked it but my father was raising his eyes. "Elvis Presley sings it," she explained afterwards and my father said seriously, "who is he while he's at home?"

"A rock and roll singer," she exclaimed, her eyes coming to life.

"Does he!" was all my father said. "Does he now, rock and roll too!"

A few more stories and songs and the night gave way. The fire was let die down. The empty bottles put back in the crate under the stairs. My mother lighting the four candles to put in the windows, to shine throughout the night, showing the way. A scrap of poetry came into my head.

A summer:
"Things bright and green, things young and happy:"

My fathers.

I went up the stairs thinking those very thoughts would be my memories too.

"Will pass and change, will die and be no more."

I looked out the window of the bathroom. It was pitch black. I couldn't see the river. But all down the road candles shone in windows. I said my prayers side by side with my father, with Patches on his other side. I lay awake watching the candlelight play on the ceiling, smelling the melting wax. Tired out I drifted to sleep between the fair head of my father at the crossroads of a summer's evening and his wet cheek one Christmas long ago. The evening sun catching the soft blue of his eyes. Only his hair was lost now. Lost like my boyhood forever.

"And I have gone upon my way
Sorrowful."

Chapter Sixteen

I went up to the cross to see the New Year in, the old year out. A new decade began. 1960 blew across my face as a bell rang. I was huddled at the Corner House with Buster, taking shelter. Tins were being banged together, a beagle-bugle sounded and people were singing, "shall old acquaintance be forgot." Buster said it was for "the sake of Auld Lang Syne." I replied drily, "it's just for the sake of keeping warm." I thought it a very strange custom to be out on such a night and I went home leaving Buster to "see it out."

Back at school again my eyes became dim. I struggled to keep up with the class. As time went on I fell behind and it was noticed by the Superior, a small, crew-out, hard-faced man. If a boy hesitated over an answer he'd get those in the seat behind to pound on his back, and those in front to attack when he twisted round. "Pound him, pound him, the pagan," he'd shout in his cruel country voice. Everybody who made a mistake was a pagan. He taught Irish of course. Writing a question on the blackboard one day he picked me out to answer it. I couldn't see a word and hummed and hawed until a flail of fists descended on my shoulders. I twisted round and I was punched from the other side. I put up my hands to defend myself but the fists were too furious and I just got to my feet. They couldn't reach me from my stand except the dentist's son who stood up. I caught his soft punch on the side of my jaw. Closing my fist I wanted to knock the superior pleasure from his pale face. Instead the Superior said sharply to him, "that's enough Paul," and I sat down seething.

I lost interest in my lessons. Only doing enough homework to get by. Spending more and more time kicking a ball and dreaming of playing for Manchester United. Listening to the older boys. On the verge of their company because I became known as a soccer player. Against the stone wall of Bawnies field, the game over, the boys gathered. Bits of talk put together in a winter's evening. The Munich crash ... the dead names spoken of in voices so low that you could only make one out by it being repeated over and over again. Duncan Edwards ... a colossus striding my imagination. New myths, only two years old.

On St Patrick's Day I wore a sixpenny badge of green with a gold harp. I went searching for shamrock for my parents the evening before. It was left to keep fresh in a jam-jar of water overnight. It was a free day and I went to half-nine Mass. Everybody was wearing shamrock and a boy asked me where was my weed. The Canon gave a sermon on emigration. I wished I was an emigrant. He made it sound as if it was our birthright.

I started missing days at school. Any morning headache and my mother's call was unanswered. By Easter I had my eyes tested at the hospital. Everybody at school had to go. The nurse put drops in my eyes and I could see through a haze. They showed me a couple of frames. The plain rimless ones were free. I didn't look beyond them. In a few weeks the frames arrived at the chemists. I knew I would never wear them. Trying them on before the mirror frightened me off them. I said I wouldn't be seen dead in them. Everybody would be laughing at me if I went outside the door. One term after Easter and I'd be away from the dread of school.

Summer came late. A bad spell started in May and never let up until the latter end of June. We were let off school a fair Friday in July. No lessons that morning, only jokes and free talk. I relaxed for the first time in ages. The empty feeling in my stomach drained away and the bunched muscles softened. The blackboard was cleaned of yesterday's work. The chalk dust drifting on the rays of the risen sun. A beautiful morning for freedom. I was away by twelve, the air, the sun and the soft blue sky was mine.

The turf was being cut out by machine now. Long tracts of bog fell under the blade. The sods were straight and heavy until the sun bent them. Once the turf was saved the lorries drove the reeks off to the generating station. The word got round that the man wanted lads to turn the turf. Buster's father told him and asked me if I'd like to make a pound. My first job and I earned ten shillings a plot. These were staked out, the sticks stood for miles. A plot looked like the size of half a football field.

Buster and I cycled up to Canburren early one Monday morning. I borrowed my father's bike and tied a turf pike along the bar. My mother packed sandwiches and a bottle of milk in a message bag. The sun rose in my face and the rich air rushed the sleep from my eyes. The road was quiet as we freewheeled down the height. Now and then a horse and cart passed on the way to the Creamery with milk. The tide was out and the river mud steamed in the heat. The sun was filtered by Carhan Wood, shooting between the branches in pins of thin light. I looked up the left turning that led to the place of my birth. It was a long time since I'd been out this way and I felt a sudden longing to see the house, now empty. Buster cycled ahead of me to attack the next hill and I had to pedal hard to catch up. I could see the slough all the way to the bottom of some hills whose names I didn't know. A few farm-houses dotted the distance. I could smell the strange white flowers growing along the banks of bog. In between the foxes fingers waved in the breeze and the black bog water reflected the sky.

Buster led me down a white dust road, passing reeks build by the side of it. Soon we were looking at the banks laden with work. Two boys from town were already turning and we stopped to ask for "the start." They had been at it a week and were expert now. Leaning on their pikes, a glisten of sweat on their brows. They showed us how to turn without breaking the length of the cut. I took the bottle of milk from my bag and sunk it in bog water to keep cool. Arranging with Buster to have lunch at twelve, I began on the third plot up. Buster walked to the fourth, his pike upon his shoulder.

It was hard lifting the soaking sods and I split the first pikeful. After a couple of lengths I got the knack and worked steadily. Sometimes I had to stop to wipe the sweat from my forehead. The early morning clouds drifted behind the hills and the sun shot free, climbing higher as the morning worked itself out. At twelve Buster beckoned and I went to get my milk. My hands were beginning to blister and I cooled them in the water. Buster was sitting on a dry clump and I found a place alongside him. My mother had put sliced banana in the sandwiches. I swapped one for Buster's tomato sandwich. The pint of milk was filling and I stretched out for ten minutes after eating.

As the day wore on the vast silence of the slough was broken. Lorries and horses and carts drove down the road, raising clouds of dust. Sometimes all that could be seen was the white dust drifting. The other two boys left early and Buster and myself worked on until hunger hurried us home. One plot. I'd earned ten bob.

I was pleased with the day as we cycled down the dust road. The way back was downhill nearly all the way. We passed a farmer bringing a rail of turf home. His horse strained against the load and the tackle jingled. He raised his whip in salute. I held my hands over both brakes all the way. Down by Carhan Wood I could smell the wild woodbine. I braked to inhale the cool scent on the evening's first breeze. The river was full, swollen with the evening tide. Its clear water flowing over the brown rocks and stones. We stopped at Carhan Bridge to watch for brown trout. We didn't delay long. I couldn't see a shrimp. The traffic was heavy on the main road, every second car was a GB. Near the horses well a gang of boys were standing, waving to the tourists.

We planned to go to the field for a kick after tea. My mother had kept the dinner in the oven. Washing my hands in the bathroom I caught myself glancing in the mirror. There was a fluff of fair hair above my lip. I had a look at my father's razor, his shaving brush, my face … my nose was red from the sun. A crop of freckles had grown on my face. I hated the sight of them. A blight on my summers. My father was delighted I was working. He placed great importance on it. "The devil finds work for idle hands," was his motto.

Buster called for me at seven, the ball under his arm. We walked down by the grotto, over the doctor's field and up the Avenue. It was a choice evening for football. A game was already on and we joined in, one on each side. Buster's side won although I headed a goal. A GAA man came down in the middle of the game but he was spotted as Buster's side were taking a goal kick. The Sergeant's son jumped high to catch the ball. I was jumping at the same time to head it and he nearly took my hair along with the ball. It was kept in the air for about ten minutes until the GAA man turned to go.

Tired and flushed I walked up town with the boys. The jukebox was playing in the ice-cream shop near the entrance to the field. Two girls were sitting on the window eating cones. We all went in for an ice-cream. Buster stood me a "99." There was a room where the jukebox played. We could sit in there and eat ice-cream while listening to the records. We trooped in and sat down on a long bench. Two girls were doing the twist in front of the jukebox. They stopped when we walked in the room and pretended to study the record names. The Sergeant's son strolled over and said something to them. They looked at each other and started to giggle. He put on a record. I listened to the words, looked at the girls and ate my "99." "Please don't treat me like a child." The girls were dressed in summer frocks and both had white cardigans. They were snapping their pointed fingers and tapping their patent shoes. I liked the deep husky voice of the singer. The Sergeant's son started an argument by saying it was a girl singing. I thought it was a big man. He said she was only fourteen. He seemed to know a lot about it. He won a "99" bet with Buster. I was amazed. She had a trojan voice for a girl. I finished my "99" and was nodding "the go" to Buster. Another record started; the pure lonely voice of that summer of 'sixty. "Jenny come lately."

The two girls looked up as we left. "You only had to smile, a little smile, nothing more than look at me." Outside, the other two girls still sitting on the window, the evening sun setting in their hair. "I only have to see the sunlight in your hair." We walked up to the Cross, not saying very much, listening to the boys talk about the girls. Always two girls. Lonely too. I could see that in the wistful turn of their eyes. On the way down from the Cross with Buster I wondered was he thinking about the Jenny of the jukebox. The evening girl with the little smile. The evening sun in her hair. Or the two girls eating ice-cream on a window sill. The two girls with the one smile in front of the jukebox. Two boys went on home, alone with their own thoughts. Their own dreams of empty evenings. Waiting for their own, "Jenny come lately."

Only the summer passed by, in lengthy days in the bog and empty evenings walking by girls sitting on window sills. Feelings near to soft rains and dreams close to the setting sun. Waiting for something to happen. A smile, a word to open my heart. Aimless in the evening after work, money in my pocket. Buster and I standing each other ice-creams, like men would in a bar. Walking out the road to the Obs. passing the girls. Always two. Silence after hello, the one word hanging in the evening breeze. Walking the summer nights, restless for no reason. Feeling welling up in my mind, changes in my body, sadness in my soul. Moving on. I had to keep moving. Going nowhere. Like the sun across the sky always to rest on the western hills. The twin hills with the dimple in the middle where the sun finally rested. The red rays racing across the river. Water gold. Image of empty life. Like the scattering of the island. The emigrant island where generations fished and farmed but now lay waste. Sheep grazing in the ruins of Beginish. The oratory lying silent on Church Island. Now they were only landmarks to the trawlers. Ancient islands that now found a rare reflection in the sky, and the silent tribute of a boy lost in the green land. The human island to the empty island, going nowhere.

Like the summer, turning to September. To end in a scatter of dead leaves on the edge of an Atlantic gale. I watched from my window, waiting for the purple hills to fade in the first fall of autumn evening. Humming the song of summer. Images of shy smiles and the sun setting in a girl's hair. And Jenny, who never came to my summer. My eyes went over the hills. The night had drawn. The hills were one: Killelan, Castlequin, Knocknadobar, Teermoyle, Beenatee. A black silhouette against the sky. My fading eyes watched the summer turn and I turned too, turned one evening to draw the curtain in my room. It was gone.

There was a poem about a boy on his way to school. I could only remember a bit of it: "Crawling like a snail, unwillingly to school." That's how I returned to school, dragging my heels behind me. All the class passed into second year; the year before the Intermediate class. The Superior told me to sit up near the front. His memory made me go red. The first day passed in writing out lists of books to buy. I bought "As You Like It" for half-a-crown from Buster. Shakespeare: Ye olde English. I looked quickly through it. I didn't like it. Buster said, "It was light reading." In the head! He was brainy, getting five honours in the Inter. The exam could be done twice but Buster skipped the fourth year.

In two years he'd have done the Leaving. Other leavings went on at home. My big sister was planning on London. She was fed up slaving for the nuns. Breda decided she wasn't going to be a nun. She left school a week after going back. She was to be a barmaid. She was fifteen and a half. My older sister was on the boat to Holyhead by the end of September. Changes. Patches passed into fifth class and he could make use of my Primary books. I couldn't fit all the extra books in my satchel so I gave it to Patches. I used Breda's. It had been thrown inside the dresser and forgotten. The hopes of my parents sprang up around me now. I was the scholar who would get a good job in the ESB or the Civil Service. Maybe a scholarship to the uni. My father urged me to mind the books or I'd finish up with a pick in my hands. They paid for the span new books without a doubt. I knew I would fail them even as I took the money. Something in the way of the village made me flinch from wearing glasses. Only the blind can measure the myths of darkness. Only the weak wear glasses. The hard man alone holds human respect and vainglory. But, glory is the teenage game, and vanity is in the winning.

The house was quiet now when I arrived home at four. Patches was leading a gang of sword fighters against invaders from New Street. The Big Terret was their battle-ground every evening after school. I teased him about it but he took it seriously enough to use a few adjectives that had nothing to do with chivalry. My mother waiting in the kitchen, her eyes vacant on the window, as if she was expecting someone. My big sister. It was in the worried furrow of her brow. She had worked in London as a young girl. She knew something. Sometimes I caught her sitting at the table in the alcove, my sister's letter open before her. Reading it again at four. I had a cup of cocoa every evening and did the maths first while the formula was still fresh in my mind. Once the maths were over with my homework was light. Maths and Latin, and my mother reading a letter from London.

On Wednesday the school had a half-day for football. Everyone had to go to the Field. Trials were held for the school team. I was second sub for the first game. It was played in Killarney and near the end the Superior wanted to take off the Sergeant's son. He asked me to go on but I told him the boy from Valentia was first sub. He went on for the last five minutes. The school lost by a goal in the last minute to the Sem. Boys were trained for the priesthood at the Seminary. I went home wondering if the day would dawn when I felt I had a vocation.

In October Buster and four boys in fifth year got jobs in the cables, in London. He told me one Friday in the Avenue. I was feeling free and fast. The news knocked the speed from my legs. I stopped with my foot on the ball. Buster going away. I thought of my mother holding a letter at four. My best friend, lost to lonely London. Walking back over the doctor's field with him for the last time I felt as if some evil force was tearing my life apart. I hid my feeling in awkward words, in silences, full of some little things we'd done together. Some game we'd won by combo. A mountain climbed. Some Saturday night film. An image of my own life. Forged in his shadow. Sundered on a Friday evening in October.

He gave me his football to keep. The white plastic with WEMBLEY written across it. Outside my door he handed it to me. I felt I was taking his greatest gift. His most innocent youth. I went in with the ball against my chest, my heart beating against it in supplication. Picturing his mother reading his letters at four o'clock, again.

He came in to say goodbye the night before he left. My

mother made a pot of tea and he sat on the sofa talking to her. Patches sat on his other side, silent for once. He didn't delay long as he was making the rounds. My mother shook hands with him at the kitchen door. Patches said "good luck" and I walked to the door with him. There was nothing to say any more. It was as if he was already a stranger. It was dark at the door and I could only see the outline of his face. He looked pale in the light from the ESB pole. The floodlights of our dreams together. He said, "see you in the summer." I answered, "all the best," and he moved from the step. I watched him walk next door. A figure on a bicycle came round the corner at Bawnies field. It looked like my father and I waited. He stopped to talk to Buster and they shook hands. My father wheeled the bike the rest of the way. He saw me standing in the door and spoke as he settled the pedal at the kerb. "It's a fright to God, they're exporting boys again!"

I asked the word that was in my mind, since I heard he was going. "Why? Why Dad?"

He stood on the step pushing his cap back on his head. "Why is it, why the republic. He was a nice obliging boy but only the child of a dream. That's the trouble with this country, all the dreams have dawned. You were the best of friends. Will you miss him?" he finished, the hard edge gone from his voice.

I said, "Yes forever," and we stood father and son sorrowing in our own ways, grieving the emigrant boy.

Chapter Seventeen

I didn't kick a ball for a week after he left. The Inter was a passport to England in my mind and there was only one leaving on my horizon. I neglected my homework, leaving the maths until I got into school. Doing them on my lap during the Irish class. School was a nightmare now; the black dread of looking at the board every morning. The long dreary nights when I couldn't concentrate and moved restlessly between my room and the kitchen. Listening to the radio, twisting the knob between Luxembourg and Radio Eireann and finding no rest at any station. Reading a library book to Patches by the open fire my mother lit in my room. It was lovely and cosy there and sometimes I'd just sit before it and close my eyes. Alone. Thinking about my future and the darkness of my eyes. Sometimes recalling Anna to my mind to keep me company. To walk with her at the end of September when the sadness fell upon the world. I had left her lying forgotten for months since her mother saw me talking to her under the ESB pole. She passed me after that, quickening her step in case I'd stop. I knew it wasn't her fault and I thought of her now as she looked the night of the races. The way she let her shoulders fall when she lost on the roulette. Her lost voice when she said, "I'm afraid to go home alone." Feeling that special night would never be mine again. Alone, thinking …

I took to walking along the old railway tracks. The wind bending the reeds that grew on the ditches. The faded yellow of the furze. The fast flow of the dykes carrying me along. Sheltered by the reaching trees. Turning up the Obs road, completing the full circle home. Sometimes I'd go up town and in the tower door of the Church to say a prayer. Five o'clock before the altar, always quiet. Only the penny candles threw any light and shadows knelt before the real presence. Kneeling to pray for any face that came to dwell in my mind, praying for my pride. When I asked myself what was I doing in the Church at five o'clock amongst the old women and their whispering of prayers, I'd pause and tell myself it was the only rest I found in the day. Home to tea; just the four of us now. Breda had her meals in the bar. It was called the White House. She started going dancing on Sunday nights, spending hours in the bathroom. Starching her dresses to stand out. Plastering lipstick on her mouth. It looked like red lead but I passed no remark. My mother thought she was growing up too soon, my father thought she was airy. Sometimes I saw her standing in the door of the bar as I passed home from school, her slight figure leaning against the doorway, a lost look on her face. I crossed over at Connor's chemist and kept my eyes to the ground for shame until I'd passed her by.

November, my birthday month, fourteen. I shaved for the first time that night. Carefully remembering how my father lathered the shaving brush with carbolic soap. Spreading the soft bristles of the brush along my chin. My face felt stiff and piercing. My father didn't use after-shave and my face was stinging all evening. I was growing up. I felt it in the nightly surges of my body. I didn't fill out at the shoulders and my frame was slender. I wished my freckles would fade away. Read in the *Sunday Press* that lemon juice was good for ridding them. I spent a whole evening in the bathroom rubbing half a lemon over my face. It only showed red and in the morning the forest of freckles was as dense as ever.

The town was getting ready for Christmas again. I heard it in the talk of turkey prices. Saw it in the bright eyes of the children looking in the shop windows. Felt it in the sudden stillness of the morning white fields. Knew it in the deeper nights. The turkey plucking started in the Creamery the December weeks before Christmas. My father had to go out after tea to kill the birds. The lorry left at a quarter to seven and picked him up at the Cross. Some of the boys from the school went out plucking, along with the men who had no work the rest of the winter. The lorries would pass back town piled high with crates of turkeys.

Their heads sticking out, crying in the night. My father often arrived home at one or two in the morning to be up again at seven. In the end the turkeys were packed and shipped off to England. A week before Christmas my father brought a turkey cock from the Creamery. He was let out the back garden to pick. My mother fed him bran to fatten him up. I helped my father pluck him on Christmas Eve.

The postman brought a card from Buster, on his last round. It was four o'clock, Christmas Eve. It was a quiet Christmas. A line of cards on the mantlepiece, the only company. The magic never touched the air. Even the sprinkle of snow gave no feeling of purity. I felt alone. I began to doubt. I didn't listen in the silent night. I went to midnight Mass. Walked there on my own in the holy night. Returned empty, under a dark sky stretching infinitely away from me. Infinite emptiness. I was just fourteen, in the season of peace, when I first felt it. Infinite emptiness.

I was counting the terms now, Easter, summer. Beyond September lay an endless, unknown time. I would leave. The thought frightened me as I walked even slower to school after the holidays. I thought the long winter nights would never have a dawn. There was dread in every waking morning. I dressed silently. I ate my breakfast in my mother's questioning silence. She sensed something was wrong but put it down to what she called "teenage troubles." She made an appointment with the eye specialist in Connor's chemist. I went up after her and found her talking to the chemist. He told me off about not wearing glasses. The specialist showed me some frames. I picked a brown pair of horn-rimmed ones. I asked him when could I stop wearing them. he said, "your eyes should be sound again when you're forty." I repeated "forty!" and he laughed. I didn't.

When the glass was fitted to the frames I went to collect them. I tried them on in my room. They didn't look too bad. I took a look out the window. Some boys were passing and I ducked behind the curtain. My father told me that I'd better wear them this time. I made no reply. He was silent for the night, reading the *Press* under the bulb. Sometimes he tried my

116

mother's reading glasses. I took the frames to school next day. It was Friday. They remained in the pocket of my bag all day and every day until Easter I put them in my bag. I couldn't do it.

There was a retreat the week before Easter. The Superior instructed the class not to talk even while in the playground. A silent week for God. The Jesuits were taking the retreat and there was a talk in the morning and again after dinner. They spoke quietly, unlike the mission where the Jesuits shouted at the congregation. There was a different subject every day and anyone in the class could suggest a topic. The sergeant's son asked the youngest priest to give a talk on teenage problems. The priest went red but he gave the talk in a shaky voice. He asked the class how many knew the facts of life. Only the sergeant's son put his hand up. He went to the blackboard and drew something. The sergeant's son was sitting next to me during the retreat and he whispered, "John Thomas." The priest faced the class and asked a country boy, "what have I drawn?" I looked again at the long shape on the board. The sergeant's son was right.

The boy was looking from the priest to the blackboard, "ah," he began ... "it's a, by God but it looks like a bit of a sally rod to me!"

The whole class started to laugh. The priest's face went a riper shade of red. "Silence!" he shouted like a Jesuit. He turned to the boy. "It's a penis," he said and the boy answered "ah," and looked at the board again after shaking his head. It was the talk of the school for the next week. Another priest gave a talk on the priesthood and gave out a pocket calendar with a prayer at the back. The Sierra prayer for vocations. He wanted boys to train in San Antonio, Texas. I dreamed of another world. He made arrangements for boys to talk to him privately if they felt they had a vocation. I wanted to see him but nobody rose that morning to go in the next room. He remained in there alone for half an hour but no one paid him a visit. The retreat was over.

A meeting was held in the library to start a youth club over Easter. Four sixth year boys organised it. I went up for a look. They got the rent of a store near the dance-hall. It opened on the first Sunday of the holidays. There was a skittle table and table

117

tennis after lunch. I paid two shillings at the door and had a couple of games of skittles. It was all boys. A record hop was held at eight that evening. I went up again and sat down to watch the dance. A row of wooden chairs lined the walls. There was an air of backward shyness in the atmosphere. Anna was there, sitting opposite me. She never got up to dance. I went home at nine o'clock. The following week I played soccer every day at three and in the evening went to the youth club. It lasted two weeks. The Canon saw a boy and a girl together outside the door the following Sunday night. The youth club was closed down because of the couple. It was said they were holding hands.

Chapter Eighteen

The last return. I felt it as I turned in the green gate of the school the first morning back. It would be the last time my stomach turned on the smell of the old stairs. The final term. The Superior gave a half-day and we had no lessons that night. Turning down a game in the Field, I went Over the Water for a walk. It was a mild day with the sky ruffled by rain clouds. I felt the reminder of the March wind at the bridge. The river was high and I watched the vicious suck of the whirlpools. Later I remembered how I shivered at the thought of being sucked to the bottom of the river. I walked all the way to Cuas Crom. Everything looked bare and cold. The hayfields, the farmhouses, the rocks by the short cut to the sea. The old castle away to the left stood green and grave above the river. Ballycarbery Castle, sacked by Cromwell, only surrendering to silence now. I took the short cut by Cahergal Ring Fort imagining life over a thousand years ago.

I could hear the rush of the waves before I reached the rise looking down over the harbour. The foam was the only break in the colour of the bay. Frothing white, the Atlantic rose to meet me. The waves crashing over the wall of the pier and attacking the cliffs that climbed above the road. I stood still, the only one living in the oblivion of the landscape. I stayed for some time, my eyes full of the sadness of the captive sea. The early evening cold started me on the road back. My mind like the swollen tide, looking for escape. If only I had the Inter I could get into the ESB I would have to leave home. Which ever way I looked there would have to be a leaving. The daylight faded quickly. The clouds thickened above the hills. It looked like a black night was threatening. I walked faster, turning up the collar of my coat. Nobody on the road. The night fell on the hills. The severe rasp of the risen wind. The dark side of the world touched me. And I going coldly home.

No storm broke that expectant night. A Christmas calm kept company with the dark. When I came home for dinner next day my mother told me of the drowning. Sometime in the quiet of the night a young fisherman walked off the pier. He was on his way to the trawler he was to work on next morning. He was seventeen; a boy from the Island. My mother said the sea was his calling.

The Guards were dragging the river for his body all morning. The trawlers stayed in shelter during the day. The fishermen gathered on the edge of the pier, waiting.

After school I walked down towards the pier. My mother told me not to go on the pierhead so I turned up the High Field, by the grotto. A huddle of boys were standing on a rock looking down. I climbed the stone wall and walked to the rim of the Terret. Below, the pier was solid with people. A guard stood at the top of the road leading down to the pier. He was stopping the children from nearing the water. I knew him. He was the young guard in the squad car. I was ten ... I walked along the rim to find a rock to perch on, for a better view. I looked out over the river. The water was sullen. A silence lay over it. A motor-boat was circling the break-water, slowly, a rope paired off from the stern. They were still searching. The trawlers were lined up by the pier tugging on the ropes. The men standing motionless on the water's edge. Waiting for the word. I looked behind me, a cluster of whispering women had taken the place of the boys on the Rock. After a while their whispers went with them as they returned home to their own children. I turned back to the scene below.

Anna walked up behind me as my eyes were lost on the water. Her voice gave me a start. "Has he been found yet?" she asked as she climbed onto the Rock. I half turned to look at her. Her face was very close, flushed. A white angora beret angled to one side of her head. A fringe framed her forehead. She was wearing a fawn overcoat and blue jeans. Her face ...

"I don't think so, they're still dragging the river," I answered quickly, running my words together.

120

"Isn't it an awful death, drowning?" she spoke without looking at me, the troubled blue of her eyes on the darkening water. I was looking out and thinking what was the idea of his life. God's will as the women would say. A boy of seventeen summers. Could it be that he felt life cold too. Last night walking down to his boat. The lonely sound of the night river. Standing on the verge of the pier. The pitch black sky above and the fathomless water in his eyes. Because he must have turned his eyes from the sky. Alone, standing on the edge of emptiness. The sea, his only calling. Did he answer?

"Isn't it?" Anna repeated, her eyes returned from the river. Looking for an answer.

"Isn't life itself an awful death?" I answered her question with my mind on the Island boy's answer.

"That's a strange thing to say," she said.

I turned to look at her, nodding to the river, "Why did he walk off there so?"

She leaned forward on the Rock and replied again without looking at me. "It's not why but how. He must have slipped" she added.

"Who can tell," I shrugged. "All we can do is ask." But not God, I thought. Don't ask Him; I knew they'd be no answer. As I was thinking the lights showed on the pier. Picking out the masts rocking on the evening tide, as if they were casting to the sky. The fishermen subdued in a shadow between two lights. The unseen sound of the motor-boat circling the silent water. I felt Anna shiver beside me. She straightened up and I saw the woman in her outlined against the night. Her face fell under a shadow and her eyes were limpid with longing on the famished Fertha. Silence. The full moon formed a crescent on the river. It shone so suddenly that I looked behind to see it hang over Beenatee. Anna brought her eyes back to me. The skylight mixed gold and silver in her hair. She smiled, biting her lower lip and I smiled without opening my lips in returned. I asked "Are you alright?" and she answered "Yes, just a little bit lonely. It's this night. The poor boy at the bottom of the river. I don't know really." She trailed off, lowering her eyes, her lashes spreading another shadow.

"I know," I said wanting to say more.

"Are you lonely too?" she surprised me with the directions of her question.

"Yes," I admitted the small word to the night. Thinking of a boy keeping vigil from a window. The September of a summer. Two girls skipping in the silent evening. A schoolgirl chant: "All she wants is gold and silver … " Her hair in the March moonlight. All I wanted was to speak my loneliness.

"I'm sorry," she said softly, without raising her eyes.

I jumped off the rock saying, "It's time to go home." Anna didn't move but I saw her shoulders hunch, then lean forward. "What is it?" I called. She turned, the moon catching her face, her eyes brimming with tears. I wanted to reach out to stop the flow, shadow her naked soul from the night. Her lips trembled with words. I couldn't hear, my eyes could only see the secret of the river reflected in the pain flooding her face. I thought I heard her say, "They've found him," repeated over and over "They've found him." Her arms crucified against the shadow thrown by the rock. Outstretched to the silver silence of the night. My legs found their strength and I clawed my way back onto the Rock. The sharp edges tore my fingers. Wordlessly Anna moved against me, her hair in my mouth, smelling of Vosene shampoo. "It's alright, don't be lonely," I was whispering thro' a lump in my throat. Her arms were light on my shoulders; the slender softness of her body warm against me. She was trying to speak again and I was saying, "I know, I know." I looked over her shoulder to the pier. The blue light of the ambulance was turning down the road. The motor-boat had stopped dragging. The trawlers were still. The fishermen were gathered round a small dark shape laid out on the grass back from the pier. A black coat thrown round it. Waiting all day for the word. Now made flesh for the silent fishermen. Water to water … dust to ,… is that the end … My arms tightened about Anna's young body; my mind screaming "no, no, no, no." I eased her face from my shoulder saying "Don't cry no more. I'm with you." Her tears had soaked my school jacket.

"I'm sorry," she said, this time clearly. "Are you going?"

I replied, "Yes," and she dropped her hands on my answer.

"Come on, there's nothing here for us," I jumped down and held out my hand. She reached down and I took her warm hand in mine. Bracing herself she dropped and steadied herself against me. This time the feel of her body awakened an answer in mine and I felt an electric tremble shoot through me. She took her hand from mine quickly and I moved back a step. Our bodies came apart as if they were burned. No word was spoken as we put the black night behind us. I glanced sideways at her face. Water still glinted in her eyes, waiting to fall. She blinked and the moonlight caught two tears on her cheeks. Wiping her face with a white hanky she looked to catch my eyes.

"I suppose you think I'm soft and silly," she said dropping her gaze.

"I do not," I said strongly. "I understand, it takes courage to cry. It's hard not to cry I mean," I added. Coming to the wall at Bawnies Field I climbed over first. Waiting for her I looked to the sky in time to see a falling star shoot downward. For a second the night flamed until the meteor vanished between the sky and Beenatee.

"A soul gone to heaven," Anna said simply from the stone wall she was resting on. I turned and smiled, reaching up to help her down. She touched my hand and jumped, her eyes bright with belief. When a star falls that means a soul has gone to Heaven; the old saying had a new hearing in my mind. I wanted to believe if only I could … Then she rested against me again and my arms went round her shoulders. She looked up into my face, a slight part to her lips. I felt my mouth go dry, heard myself say "Are you happy now?" and her lips shone wetly in the light from the sky. She spoke softly, "Yes, always with you," and I drew her close bending my mouth to meet her opening lips. Her arms crept round my neck and I felt the soft strain of her breasts through her coat. I took my mouth and pressed my cheek to hers.

"We better go now," I said in her ear.

"Yes, in a minute," she whispered, her warm breath brushed my face. We held ourselves in silence for a while. She stirred first saying "you know we saw the falling star tonight."

"Yes, I know," I hugged her.

"Well, I have fallen too," she added and my heart skipped a beat on her words. I waited in wonder. Over her shoulder I could see the Marian. Home, and above the Rock, the border between me and the sky beyond Beenatee. I thought strangely of Johnny. He could never hold her and I was ashamed at the thought. My arms pressed her tightly.

"For you," she was saying. "I have fallen. I love you." I raised my head to look at her face. Her eyes were moist again and her lips parted to show the shine of her front teeth.

I heard myself say, "I've loved you since the night of the roulette," and she raised her lips to kiss me softly. I felt her teeth this time and I wanted to open the front of her coat. We came apart after a long time, my body shaking. The teenage dream came true for me in that moment as we walked hand in hand down the height of Bawnies Field. We parted at the ESB pole in the square. Before she reached up to brush my lips lightly she told me. "I cried tonight because I was thinking of my twin brother. He was drowned too. He was only eight." My mind went cold.

I said, "I know, I'm sorry. I knew him too."

"Wasn't he your special friend?" she asked.

"My best friend," I said the words as if they were foreign to me. She was looking sad again.

"He'd be happy for us tonight," she said and I kissed her quickly in answer. I watched her slight figure until she faded in her front garden. I turned my back on the night. Alone at ... I couldn't think. My mind was faced with time. I was living outside myself. Nothing was real. I wondered what time it was. I ran from the memory of another night. Turned my back. Alone at ... Alone.

Chapter Nineteen

I couldn't eat breakfast next morning for thinking of her. I looked out over the river from the bathroom. The light tumbling down over the hill rolling the river with a faint brightness of blue. Morning calm lay heavily over it. Innocent of the night, as if it never laid claim to life. I saw a trawler put out by the headland along Bosses Strand. A meadow in the summer. Strange how I longed for a gather of gold. Shutting the bathroom window I went downstairs to collect my bag. School was full of rumours. Someone said the body found in the drag wasn't the boy from the Island at all. I listened and thought about last night. The restless wander of my mind before sleeping. Then the sleep that held no rest and the morning that I moved through contained cold.

At dinner my mother was talking about it to my father. Making brown gravy and conversation. Mary had told her the story at the Cross. A skeleton body of a boy, a very young boy, had been hauled in. The fish had fed on his flesh; the sea had turned him green. He had been dead for a good many years. The Guards thought he was the boy that went missing six years back. His parents were being asked to identify the body. All that remained were tufts of fair hair over the memory of a smiling face. Blue eyes that shone like stolen stars at the bottom of the river. The sky had turned with his loss. I had trampled on the fallen star. His only remains. My mother was asking me again, "Didn't you remember him? He used to scald me calling for you at all hours, the scut. A manly piece, who could talk till the cows came home. But a lovely boy all the same. Don't you remember?"

"No," I said and got up from the table, my dinner untouched. "I didn't." My father looked up and I held my eyes away from him. They watched me go and I walked back the Avenue to pass my dinner break. In the yard outside the barracks cars were lined up. Guards were everywhere; walking cycling, driving. I turned my face away, walking fast towards the Avenue Road. The squad car was coming down, I stepped in near the wall. A face looked hard at me; her mother's, lean and tight. Her eyes pierced me and I clutched the wall till my hand hurt. The car crawled past before I realized the Sergeant had saluted me. That move of a blue arm made me feel better. They must be on their way to name the body. I hoped it wasn't him. Thought back to see if I could remember any other drowning. Only the football team from Valentia and they were men. Thought back ...

To walk, if I could keep walking I might forget. I kept right away from the school, back New Street and out Valentia Road. I couldn't return to school. To be alone, if I could be alone I might forget. I walked and walked until I reached the Points Cross. Turning right toward the Point, a slipway to Valentia. The ferries anchored there to transport the Island people home. Two miles down; the uncut bogs on the left and the neglected fields on the right. A grey slough settled into the far hill, beyond the bog. A deserted house stood bare on the side of the road, close to the Point. Windows smashed and the roof running to green. No setting sun would ever reflect gold on that house. No boy would dream of climbing a hill to follow. I arrived at the Point and stood on the slipway to look across at the Island. A ferry was pulling out and I could hear the engine above the swell of the waves. I watched it cross at a tangent, its bow dipping and rising in the water. A man wearing an Aran jumper and cap was the cox. An old couple sat in the bow clutching a roll of rope. The ferryman helped them off, steadying the boat with one hand on a bollard by the slipway. "Are you bound for the Island?" the man was asking me. I roused myself.

"No, no I amn't thanks," I smiled.

"Righto, good luck anyway," he called pushing off again.

"Safe crossing," I shouted into the wind. He waved and I watched him to the far shore.

I spent the day walking back along the old railway. School was out when I reached the bottom of the Marian. Blessed myself passing the grotto. Met the Sergeant's son playing soccer in the square. I didn't mind talking to him. He never mentioned the drowning; only wanted to talk about soccer and women. He brought my bag home. The Superior wanted a note about my absence. While talking I kept an eye on Anna's house. The light was on and the kitchen curtains drawn. The Sergeant's son was about to go home for his tea. I walked up town with him. He nudged me passing the green garages opposite the old graveyard. My initials and Anna's were chalked up. Childish. I suddenly grew above abbreviated life. It didn't bring a blush to my cheeks as before. I answered him with a small smile. At the Cross I parted company with him. Walking up the Main Street I took the time from the Chemist clock; five o'clock. I turned in the silver gates of the church and round by the back door. Dusk and silence mingled with a fresh smell of incense. Sinking candles threw a line of light across the statue of Our Lady. The bare shadow of an old woman knelt before the altar. I genuflected and turned softly left to the mortuary. I could make out the shape of a coffin on the ... blue ... small ... and I was running through the door and into the cool rush of wind. I walked home because there was no place else to go. No mention was made of the day. My mother had a note ready next morning. I walked to school and didn't care what the sarcastic Superior might say. The day passed away; staring out the window, my eyes on the silent sky.

Evening, my mother reading a letter from London, four o'clock by the window light. Took off her glasses and told me. "The boy was buried today, in a little blue coffin. Only the family went in the funeral. Their poor minds are at ease at last, six long years in limbo, his mother must have suffered. Here, drink your cocoa before it gets cold. What got into you yesterday?" she asked as I was sipping my drink. "I don't know, the drowning maybe. I'm going back to the Avenue," and I drained my cup.

I met her coming down the Avenue Road and my heart stopped. Her eyes were red-rimmed. She stepped up to me and I said, "hello." There was nobody about.

She said, "I'm glad to see you today," and she was very

close.

I took her hands, "I'm sorry about ..." and her hair muffled my words. I held her, pressed her back to the shelter of the wall.

"I know you are," she was crying. "I know you are." Did she, I asked myself, did she know? She eased me away. "I'm sorry, I must go home. My mother is expecting me. I'll see you tomorrow after school," and she was gone.

"After school," I repeated and she waved.

Putting out in the ebb tide that evening, Mary's brother bumped the body of the Valentia boy. He was lying face down against the breakwater. After an inquest he was taken home in the trawler he used to work on. He lies buried in the Island graveyard, and buried in the depths of my darkness forever.

Many times after school since then, waiting at the Chemist Corner for me. The sensitive profile of her face framed in the mirror on the window. Some days she'd walk up as far as the library and wait by the railings. We'd both walk down by the bridge, over to the Lawn. Not touching but close together. Talking about inconsequential things, just to hear the soft murmur of her voice. She kept me warm when the cold feeling of lonely took me away from my home. When the inexplicable restlessness made me walk for miles alone. To feel the deepest silence and return with nothing in the world to touch me. Neither the spring stirring in the earth gave hope, nor the wild flower of the fields. The cuckoo in the wood. I passed the spring by, neither grieved or sung for its labour.

The days lengthened and the leaving cut to weeks. The school was preparing to celebrate its centenary. Photos of every class were taken on the lawn of the monastery, in Bridge Street. I wore my best jumper with the grey cross-over neck. The Bishop of Kerry called and we all had to form a guard of honour and clap him. A play called "Miss Eire, I am Ireland" was put on in the dancehall. I was singing and had to learn the words of the National Anthem in Irish. The play centered round Patrick Pearse and the 1916 rebellion. The dentist's son was taking the part of Robert Emmet and his tinny voice shook with feminine fervour when he reached the only part of the speech I remembered; "And when my country takes its place among the nations of the world, then and not till then let my epitaph be written." He died for Ireland. For illusions I thought. Everybody clapped and the choir sang "The Three Flowers," the symbolic trinity of the Republic. Robert Emmet, Wolfe Tone, Patrick Pearse and I thought of a white-haired old man. The flowers wither but their memory would never die. White gravel on a graveyard and the white cross at the side of a lonely road. History repeated. The National Anthem and the hall was on its feet, facing the Tricolour. I wiped the red make-up from my cheeks and drank the bottle of lemonade each boy got for his part.

A magazine was produced of the one hundred years. The Superior expected every boy to buy a copy. It had a pure white cover and articles about old times in the school by past pupils. My mother thought it was an expensive century. But when I bought it for the reluctant eight and six she didn't put it down all night. I read the review of the pageant in the paper: A pageant, *The Felons of our Land* was presented on Wednesday, Thursday and Friday by pupils of the CBS. Verse speakers unfolded the story while a choir of 50 voices gave a stirring rendering of appropriate ballads and songs with glorious intonation and precision. The pageant was presented in four scenes:—

    I   Introduction
    II   Perchance to Dream
    III   An Ambition Achieved
    IV   Surrender but not Defeated

Its main theme was the patriot martyr Patrick H Pearse and the 1916 Rebellion. An epilogue was written to the Centenary pageant. Epilogue was like evening; at the end of the day. At the end of the story ...

Chapter Twenty

Summer came slowly; the evenings stretching with the sun. The hills lost their grey coat. The furze and heather blew wild on the brush of the wind. The air dried, smelling of sun and sea. The river turned and mirrored the blue of the sky. The May Missions began early. A stall selling scapulars and rosary beads, holy medals and statues of every saint going was erected above the church. It was the women's week first and my mother and Breda left each evening at a quarter to eight. Jesuits: fire and brimstone and the seven year plan. Given a child before the age of seven the Society would determine the man he was to be.

I went the second week, sitting at the front of the church. My father stayed down near the back door, in the "Reserved for men" seats. He enjoyed their sermons and stories, their voices dropping dramatically from the mountain to the mute. Man. The memory between earth and eternity. And life: a road with no name. A man with no memory for the road is a lost soul. I listened to the words falling in the evening silence, a rainbow across the altar. The sun diffused on the cross bathing the abused Son with its broken liquid light. And the words kept falling and my mind picked them up, put them together to build a way. The *via dolorosa* where pride and pain keeps company. At the end of the evening when the priest was silent and the sun fell behind the hill, when the church bowed in benediction I closed my eyes. Dark. A road. No name. A memory. I. And words falling like my faith, falling away from me. I walked home alone, the May night around me, its warm darkness closing me off from the doubts of day. I drank my cocoa, laughed with my father when he mentioned a joke the Jesuit made during the sermon. Went upstairs and leaned out the window of my bedroom. Inhaling the dark air of the heather hills. Watching the summits making a black circle against the night sky. Sounds of children in a hunt reached my window. Reflected my own young night. Echoed my own, unbroken voice. Saddened my soul that echoes and reflections were only repeated illusions. "Ink, ank under the bank, Ink ank out." Out. Every day of my life was counted. Add them up and get the wrong answer. Because how many silent nights, like tonight, will go with my days. I looked again to the sky; suffused with blue, the evening star, and immense emptiness. I could feel it, almost physical inside me. My heart contracted, my stomach felt light. "There is no One there." My mind was forming actual words. Falling words like falling stars. Old folks' fable. Myth not meaning. There is no One there. I abruptly closed the window. Took off my clothes and went to bed for the first time in my life without going on my knees. Night prayers now felt like nightlines to the stars, to me. Lying awake a long time I wondered what my parents would think if they knew I didn't believe any more. For evermore. I slept in the end, the night dying and the morning at the wake.

June. The Leaving and the Inter. The school in a state of revision for weeks. The teachers, concentrating on the exam classes, neglected us with freedom. The time of my life running out. I didn't think about leaving any more. The summer holidays would be the time to forget the idea of school. Exams and futures failed to intimidate my indifference. I just packed my school-bag every night. Walked into the musty classroom every morning. Played soccer on Saturday. Went to Mass on Sunday. "Friday night is my delight, and so is Saturday morning. But Sunday noon it comes too soon for school on … Monday morning." The last week. It felt strange when I walked in the green gates that Monday. Eight years and two below in Bridge Street at Brother Barrett's. The infant's academy which taught me the first lesson of life. If I had to take a legend from school now it would be the ageless man everybody knew simply as Brother Barret. When the years would erase the memory of all my teachers who stood before the blackboard, one remained; he gave his time to me, and his time was eternal.

When the day was spent I loitered on the way home. Wanted

to see her waiting by the library for me. The library gate hung open; a child swinging to and fro. The street was aloud with the language of children. Calling, teasing and hunting each other around cars and ESB poles. But she wasn't there. I didn't have absolute arrangements to meet her. Sometimes she had to go home for her mother. Those days were no days to me. Today was wished into tomorrow. I looked out for her at the Chemists. Only the memory of her profile in the mirror as I passed. Across the street a gang of country school-girls made remarks from outside the Irish House. I looked away, down Railway Street. A group of old people shuffled impatiently outside the doctor's surgery. The convent school was still emptying in ones and twos. The dark blue uniforms emphasising the dreary day. The street ahead held no trace of her. Looked empty and alien. Unknown in my faded eyes. Everything looked like an outline. Even the names on the shop widows looked like foreign letters. I knew it wasn't just the weakening of my eyes. I was travelling on the road home and each step was heavier than the last. To know when I reached the door that I was further than ever from rest. Thoughts of another home raised my eyes to the hills. The ever present curtain where I once peeped through to see the golden illusion of innocence. The face of Johnny's mother came before me, the longing for home in her eyes, wet behind a torn curtain. Long ago … when I longed for a home under the stars. I wondered was the restlessness I felt just the tinker in my soul. Would I wander forever and find no home?

I never set eyes on her that evening. Night, after tea sitting in my room, the early twilight on the window. The radio turned to Luxembourg. Shadows deepening on the walls of the bedroom. My eyes closed, silence in my mind. My father coming up and finding me, saying "What are you doing in the dark?" and turning on the light without drawing the curtain.

"Nothing," I answered shortly and he was taken aback.

"Nathing," he repeated and I corrected him by repeating, "Nothing," distinctly.

"You're a good hand at that lately."

He pulled the curtain and I felt strangely trapped. He continued "I haven't seen you open a book this past month.

Haven't you any lessons to do?" I sat up resentfully.

"No," I answered turning the radio up.

"Turn that thing off," his voice was cutting. I switched it off and waited, my eyes on the floor. "Listen here to me," his voice sounded severe. I listened, "Maybe you've no books to learn," he began and I was on the point of contradicting him. Books to learn. He must think the teachers were all Beano brains. He was going on ... "but there's plenty of work to be done in the bog, you can start footing tomorrow evening. If your brother is willing to do it, so should you. You're old enough and big enough not to mention idle enough for it; you can take the bike." He stopped and I could feel his eyes on my head. "Do you hear me?" he asked in the silence.

"Yes," I replied without looking up.

"Make sure you do." I heard him turn and walk out of the room.

My hands were shaking when I reached out to turn the radio back on. His voice, hard and country, embarrassed me. The way he said "nathing" for "nothing". The possession in the way he told me to go up footing the turf, as if he owned me. Getting up I made for the bathroom. Voices drifted up the landing as I went by, one raised, one insistantly soft. His and my mother's. I knew they were talking of me. Without hearing a word I sensed the calm support of my mother. She tried to understand my need to be alone. I washed my burning face under the cold water tap. Opened the bathroom window and took a breath of summer scented air. Newly cut grass and the ancient smell of turf mixed a memory in the night. I closed the window and went back to my room. The radio was announcing the news. I switched it off and walked slowly downstairs for my cocoa. The front door shut as I reached the coarse mat at the bottom. My mother in the scullery, Patches curled up in the sofa, reading. My father's footsteps ringing off the concrete. I could tell his step on any strange street, an echo that was fading away from me. Strange.

Evening in the darkening silence of the bog. The midges picking away at me. Stooping to foot the brittle dry turf. Pains bending my back as the night came. Loneliness stretching across the empty, endless slough, meeting the foothills and reaching to the top where the sombre sky began. As soon as darkness fell fully I was gone. Hopping on the bike and pedalling madly from the lonely night.

Friday. Fish and the *Kerryman* … and my last day. Doing every little thing for the final time; going through an ordinary day. Dawning blue above Beenatee and dying in an image of autumn. In between I walked slowly in the green gate. Songs and jokes and my silences. Staring blindly at the blackboard. Yesterday's lessons still chalked up, still unlearned. The Superior giving the class a brief lecture on civics for the summer. The Angelus bell. Impatient prayers. The excitement of summer raising voices round the classroom. The final word "dismissed." I found myself at the top of the musty stairway to the outside world, sweeping the playground with a quick glance. Echo of concrete and crayon and some crying. Out the passage way leading to the green gate. I turned to look back, too many movies in my mind. Alma Mater. Old and yellow and dying on the side of the road. In that last moment I despised her. Called down drab reality on her dreams. Turned away into the chanting street:

> "No more Latin,
> No more French,
> No more sitting on a hard old bench."

No more. A day divided into stretches of time. Dawning blue above Beenatee, and dying in an image of Ireland. Like me and my Alma Mater, partitioned by pride. Sunset on the Republic of Dreams.

Chapter Twenty One

Night. Awake in my room. Warm dusk at the window. My eyes open and restless on the ceiling. Patches's breathing disturbing the stillness. The Marian asleep: the hills, sentries in shadow under the night sky. "All's well with the world," and me keeping watch over its darkness.

I never mentioned the leaving to my parents, meaning to at tea-time but my father sent me up to the bog. One more bank and it would be all footed. A week of drying weather and I'd be drawing it out to the road. There, it would be clamped into the big reek. Then my evenings would be free for soccer. A street league was being organised; seven-a-side. They were still playing in Bawnies Field when I returned from the bog. The Wembley ball bright and white under the light from the ESB pole on the corner. The boys making the most of their first day of summer freedom.

Silent summer. I would pass through it, holding my secret to it's shadows. In the mornings I got up at nine. Drawing the curtain from the brilliant blue sky. Throwing open the top and both sides of the window. Warm waves of wind. Waking Patches and sitting on the side of the bed planning the day. Mending the puncture in my sister's bike with a patch and solution. Dipping the tube in a bucket of water to see if there was a bubble of air. Giving Patches a carrier to Cuas Crom. The river shallow as we cross the bridge. Hot tar sticking to the tyres as I struggled up the Lawn height. The road and the day stretching far ahead. Farmers saving hay with the morning sun. Stopping to lean on their haypikes after waving at us. The tourists out early. A French car stopping, asking was it far to Dingle. Before I'd time to tell the driver Patches piped up, "You'll never row to Dingle in that class of boat." The

135

Frenchman had to be convinced there was a road to Dingle. Laughing in the young morning, down the short cut by the stone fort. Meeting the road to Cuas Crom and Patches rising on the carrier. Cool water, calm and sunless in the shadows cast by the cliffs. At the far side of the sea, blue mountains, a shade below the sky. Nobody in sight, just a farmhouse above the harbour. Cattle grazing. A white coat of sheep on the outcrop of the cliffs.

I visited the cold caves, water trickling down the walls. Looked down between the rocks for crabs to humour Patches. Raced along the short sand in my bare feet. Paddled up to my knees in the sharp water. The sun, deep into the day, told me the time. Home to cups of spring water, cooling my cheeks under the cold tap. Reading the *Press* out in the back after dinner. Off again to the White Strand to play football. Cars on the slipway; children building castles. Voices breaking over the white waves, sea surging relentelssly for the shore. Cattle gadding from the flies, making for the shallows at the end of the Strand. Standing mourn-faced in the heat of the day flickering their tails. Patches building two goals with sand. Sweat dribbling down my forehead. Buster's ball dribbled at my feet. Drinking the big bottle of orange and water my mother gave us. Lying dreaming in the sun … Cars began to leave; five o'clock. Giving Patches odds and racing him to the bike. Freewheel down the height, the salt air piercing my sunburned neck. Passing children thumbing home. Bicycles two abreast, filing to one on the hoot of a car. Red faces and tanned thighs of the girls. The boys shaping off in front of them; freewheeling without hands. A priest passed, his car full with waving children. The Creamery manager flew past without a nod. I could see him every day swimming in Cuas Crom. It made me wonder why my father worked seven days a week. I was glad when I got to the top of the Lawn height. Patches was beginning to weigh.

Seven o'clock and I was making for Bawnies. Football to forget. Dribbling with the outside of my foot. Attempting feats of fantasy. Running, running to feel free, vying with the wind. Poised for speed in front of goal. Scoring with a header in the first half. My shirt sticking to my back, my face and neck rolling with salt. Light fading as the sun went down. The ball a blur skimming over the black grass; narrowing my eyes to see a cross from the right wing. Instinct controlled the ball on my right foot. Side-stepped a slide tackle and hit it on the volley with my left. Game ball. The night on the field.

Summer nights when the game was over. Up town to the milk bar; the smell of ice-cream and still orange. The girls in their summer frocks sitting close together. The boys in a standing huddle, pretending that the girls weren't there. Some nights Anna was sitting quietly, sipping orange. Talking to her friend from up town. Raising her eyes to glance at me when no one was looking. Touching her with my eyes, her bare brown thighs showing as she crossed her legs. The rigid rise of her breasts as she got up to buy two 99s. The night breeze cooling my face at eleven when the bar closed. The walk home in her wake; the boys breaking up at the Cross. Some of them continuing to walk aimlessly up town. Would walk and walk from East End to Valentia Road, islands all. On towards midnight and off home. In Anna's nights I would turn down at the Cross. Catch her slow footsteps up and walk in the shadows of the old graveyard with her. Past the green garage where her initials and mine were carved. Sometimes laughing, at times silent with each other. Building bridges in the night. My shoulder brushing against her; she shouldering me playfully back. Acting with our bodies the young needs of the night. In the total darkness of the tower the silent silhouette of her body turning to me. My hands reaching out, called from silence by the expectant part of her lips. Shadow to shadow, moulded to the stones, the night and our bodies, one. Her thin blouse and dress retaining the warm day. Smelling of sea and salt. Stealing kisses from the night, coming apart on the sound of footsteps. Flushed, walking into the light of the ESB pole. A man calling "goodnight," and I late in answering, my mouth still full of the feel of her lips. No lingering under the light in the square. Just a quick goodbye and promise of the White Strand tomorrow.

Another day. Getting up late. Walking to Dom's for the paper. The sun in my eyes and her face on my mind. Dom delaying me to talk about Manchester United. Special even out of season. Envied England for their unique United. Mulling over something Dom said on the way down with the paper: "If we had a United Ireland we wouldn't need to dream of Man United." I'd be up to him again Saturday, for a haircut. He could talk on any subject under the sun and a few above with it.

Patches was kicking the ball against the front of the house when I rounded the corner. He was aiming at the four squares of glass on the front door for practice. My mother at the window reading the riot act and he laughing, pretending to kick the ball at her. "Will you take him over to Bawnies out of the way. He's my heart scalded this blessed morning," my mother implored as I pushed the kitchen door open with the paper. I thought it a bit warm for running but went dribbling up the road, with Patches trying to tackle me. For an hour we played a goal to goal match along the ground. I let Patches win to make up for telling him I wouldn't be carrying him to the Strand after dinner. When the game petered out we sat down on the burning grass, watching the road. The women strolling up town for the morning messages. Stopping to chat, unhurried, "the day's long." My mother was going to get Patches a new pair of sandals on Saturday. Last year's sandshoes were still a good fit for me.

Lazy breeze on my face. Smell of green growth. My head propped on the Wembley. The sun reaching down to close my eyes. A bee buzzing from flower to wild flower. Patches incredibly calm. The trees in the old graveyard at rest. The world slowly slowing down. Timeless. Sun sleep. Patches woke me as my father was coming down the road, walking between the other two Creamery men. I would always see the three men walking down that road. One o'clock, I got up and ran with Patches, jumping on the wall and onto the gravel at the side of the road. Handing the ball to one of the men to solo. Having a kick-up in the square.

At a quarter to two my father walking up to the Cross to meet the Creamery lorry. My mother washing the dinner ware in the scullery. Patches solo-ing the ball around the ring. "Not a splink," my mother muttering as she looked out to see what blackguarding he was up to. Packing milk 'n' water with a packet of Mikado biscuits into the old message bag. Pumping the bike until I couldn't press the tyre. Taking the pump with me for fear of the slow puncture. Cycling down by the grotto by two o'clock. The promise of the night before me; the day would keep. The river looked spent and glazed. Only the rare ripple rushed to unsettle the solid blue.. The bridge bright with young people. Cycling and walking; some sitting, some thumbing. Cars crawling carefully over the narrow span. One boy fishing off a column; the rod twice his size. His eyes dedicated to the intense water.

Straining up the Lawn height; determined not to have to walk, like the girls. Off the saddle; blessing myself past the graveyard. Looking down on the town opposite, like a wayward Y drawn on a green page. I was side-by-side with home, parallel to peace. Didn't anyone feel like I felt? Different. Strange doubts that it's all a dream. That when I looked at the blue sky I only saw the expression of my own eyes. Diffused in the light of the four winds. A scattering of seed without a hope of harvest. I turned my mind to the fertile fields. At least they would realize the emerald reality. Haycocks dotted both sides of the road. A distant field of wheat shimmered without a sound. A breeze played on the reeds by the side of the road, shaking them into song. My father had a favourite tune called the "Stack of Barley." He loved to dance to it at weddings and socials. I thought Stack of Barley a ridiculous title, but I saw the dance today. I almost turned down the grass road to the Castle. The grim-looking National School stood at the top of the road, looking down timidly on the skyward Castle. "Kimego National School," straight out of the 19th century. The road ahead ... rock and furze at the turn to Cuas Crom. The triangle of a sloping hayfield cut from the poor land. A farmer making wynds, waving his hayrake in salute. I raised my hand in return thinking that his triangle was more than I would ever own of this earth. Coming to the short cut to Leacanbuile Fort, I passed by the ninth-century shrine.

Colour and cloud, sunshine and shadow. Sounds drifting to the shore, silences ebbing to the sea. Foam dancing off the rocks and a young boy diving into white furry. I put on the

brakes to freewheel slowly down. The smell of the sea air
strengthening in the wind. Resting the bike against the worn
wall, still sitting on the saddle. My legs balancing on the
ground, scanning the length of the far pier. No recognition of
her name on the carrying breeze. The shouts and messages sent
and brought by others. I couldn't decide whether to hold or go.
Cars and bikes raised dust like a convoy down the road. I
waited until the road settled. Turned and pedalled fast to make
the long height, leaving the chaos of colour behind me. Took
the grass short cut to the White Strand. The country was full of
short cuts, I thought. Short cuts and long wounds. The open bay
before the White Strand smelled of stale seaweed. Two young
boys were searching for periwinkles between the rocks and the
smooth round stones. Sea shells and the scattered dots of white
stones dazzled my eyes. A cyclist passed at the top of the
height, then descended like a rolling rock. A girl in blue jeans,
her dark hair flying in her wake. Slowing on the level, she
called out something as she passed. Her words broke into
silence, but I didn't understand them. It was only when I caught
a lightening glimpse of the face that I could tell it was Anna's
friend from up town. I looked over my shoulder to see if she'd
stop but she was facing the signpost to Cuas Crom. I thought of
turning round but the White Strand was only over the top of the
height.

Chapter Twenty Two

The White Strand. White with the definition of distance. The nearer I approached the more the grey sands became apparent. The tide was coming in, the waves creeping and crashing to the shore. A solitary car was parked on the slipway, three bikes rested in the shade. I put the bike behind the car and walked without hurry into the warm soft sand and down to the water. I strolled along the shoreline, side-stepping the water as it expanded. One child playing on the sand, alone on a castle without care. A man and a woman sitting on a blanket by the sand-dunes. Cattle in a cluster over by the cool rocks. Two young boys swimming against the tide without an idea of danger. The car and two bikes accounted for. I watched the shoot of white rise against the blue background of the sky, behind the little islands. I walked over by the rocks; the baleful eyes of the animals never left me as I climbed to the soft green grass. In my view above the bay I saw the twin hills rising yellow with flower. Tracing the rim of the sky with a coarse finger of furze. To my left a stretch of land was wired off down to the beginning of the first rocks. The sea shaped the land in a wide curve that turned up river. A fair figure coming into view in the distance. Body balancing on a massy stone. Tight breasts pointed in profile against the white spray. Her face thrown back to catch the sun coming off the water. I raised myself to my knees to get a better look. She was dressed all in blue. Except for her fair hair she could be part of the sea and sky. I screwed up my eyes but could barely trace the outline of her face. For a minute I was frightened that my eyes were losing their light. I watched her skip from rock to rock, her hair blowing across her face. Frightened to face the cattle she veered up towards the fence. I lost sight of her but heard her slapping the rocks with her sand shoes. Her hair rising from the rocks. Shining with gold where the sun caught the loose strands. I wanted to rise and run. The butterflies had disappeared from the fields and were fluttering in my stomach. My heart started and stopped and wild blood raced through my veins. My mind was picking out random words to put together. I was alone on an empty beach, the day held no escape. I was swimming in the startled depths of Anna's wide blue eyes.

"Hello," she said quietly, without smiling. "You gave me a start," she gave a little laugh. The lashes fell down over her eyes like a cloud across the sky.

"Sorry, I didn't mean to." I lifted her eyes with my voice. She looked down on me, her lips curved over her teeth in a pout. Suddenly she sank to her knees in a slow feline fall.

"I'm puffed out," she sighed sitting on the backs of her thighs.

"It's no day for endeavour," I spoke with my eyes racing along the shore. In reply she dropped her shoulders in the child-like way I loved. I lay back on an elbow and asked her, "Is your friend coming back? I passed her at the bottom of the height."

She pulled her legs straight to sit close to me. "No, she's off to meet the new banker's two daughters in Cuas Crom."

"Another new one!" I exclaimed. "They're not a very good mint," I added with a smile towards her. She smiled with her eyes in returned and said, "they don't last as long as Foxes." We both burst out laughing as she pulled a silver bag of Foxes mints from her jeans. She held the bag out to me and the awkward ice melted in her warm smile.

I told her I had milk and Mikado to eat first. She had left her sandwiches in a sand dune and I said, we could have a picnic. Her eyes lit up and she jumped to her feet in delight. A child of woman smile played around her lips. I raised myself slowly to my feet and felt the nearness of her. Racing over the dunes, her blue-clad body by my side. Jumping through the air into the burning sand. Around lay the burrows, like black eyes, where the rabbits hid. Sitting on her bath towel, propped against the bank of the dunes; drinking milk and water and sharing the Mikado. I took one of her ham sandwiches, the butter melting in my fingers. The wind whistled when I held the empty bottle up. She cleared up when all the food was eaten, clearing the crumbs from the towel.

I lay back and she looked down, her hair framing her face. A bead of sweat crossed her forehead and trickled down her cheek. I reached up and brushed her face. It was warm and warmer where I touched. Her eyes seemed to widen and her cheek pressed against my hand. I wanted to be gentle. I cupped her other cheek with my free hand and drew her face down. The shadow of her hair fell across my eyes. I could feel the soft waves against my cheeks. Her lips were moist and open as they came down on my mouth. My hands left her face and pulled her shoulders against me. The length of her soft body lay on top of me. Her pointed breasts flattening on my chest, her thighs between my open legs. My hands played up and down her back as we kissed. I opened her teeth with my tongue. Deeper and deeper I explored her moist mouth. Without taking my mouth away I turned her on her back. I could feel the hardening of her breasts through the blue top. My hand found the heaving mound. She moaned and tried to tear her mouth from mine. My hand slipped under the bottom of her tee shirt. Her bare skin was warm and my hand burned on the touch of her breast. I felt the hard tip of her nipple, my thumb kneading it to stand out. She was struggling in earnest. Her mouth tore free. "No, no, please don't. It's a sin." A sin? My body was blazing with her feel. My hand was still under her top. She was near to tears as her hands grabbed my hidden hand and pulled it down over her flat stomach and out into the sun. I fell off her, breathing strongly. Shame reddened my cheeks. I couldn't look at her face. No word had been spoken. A bead of sweat on her cheek and my innocent hand reaching out. I wanted to be gentle …

"I'm sorry," I said looking quickly at her. She was pulling her tee shirt down over the top of her jeans, her breasts eagerly pushing out their peaks. My look lingered until she caught my eye and answered. "It's not all your fault." Her voice sounded small and far away. "We'll have to ask forgiveness, that's all."

"I'm not confessing," I replied sharply. The sun was still blazing down but I felt cold. The day had brought changes. I had played with innocence and lost. Was to her an occasion of sin. Deny my own guilt to her face. To the shiny face of God. "You'll never make a good confession if you don't," she answered, her eyes turned down.

"Does one other confession matter?" I argued. "I haven't made a good confession in years, six years," I added.

She raised her eyes and laughed low saying, "you may think you were an old man the way you talk. Six years ago you had barely passed the age of reason."

"How could you make a bad one, you're as innocent as the green grass at eight."

"That's what you think," I mumbled. "The young grass isn't always green." She was silent for a moment gazing out over the dune. "What about the young grass that gets cut? My brother? Was he innocent at eight?" My blood went cold.

"How should I know about him?" I cut the word out.

"Why have you gone pale?" she kept her voice calm. "I suppose you deny him like you deny God? Were you ever my brother's keeper," she questioned.

"Keeper?" I tried to make little of her. "I admit I've played in goal for him, but ..." She didn't even smile, just stared in front of her. "I'm sorry, I didn't mean to make fun of you," I stopped carrying the catechism last Easter. I'm nobody's keeper, nobody's," I emphasised. She swung her hair over her shoulder with her two hands. She was not a girl any more but a woman.

"I'm sorry too, sorry for you. You've lost your faith and way. If you ever want to tell me why I'll be there. I'll always listen because you know I'll always love you," she spoke softly, her voice tremulous. I eased myself close to her and she threw her arms around my neck. I held her without touching her body, my hands tangled in the warm softness of her hair. No word was spoken; I closed my eyes and pressed my cheek to the side of the head. Wanted that moment of softness and silence to keep in memory forever.

I was weeping with words, words that wanted to empty my mind. I wanted to pour out the bitter torrent of mood and memory. Wash the sin of silence from my soul. Find peace in the fullness of time. Time was my trial, if I could face it. If she could forgive ... Weeping words into the curtain of the confessional. Confiteor. The priest drawing the Latin light across my bowed head: "Ego te absolvo." Kneeling to say my penance before the Blessed Sacrament. Out into the summer evening. Innocent as the green grass. Her young hand slipping softly into mine. Her hair, diffused gold from the sinking sun. September would never again season my sadness. Words. All I could say was, "Anna, Anna." After a time I eased my head away and looked in her face. She smiled, a lost smile, her shoulders fell in her girlish way. I squeezed her shoulders quickly and spoke. "Not today, but some time I will tell you. Because if I can't talk to you, who is there to listen?"

"I ..." she began, but I closed her lips with my fingers.

"No," I shook my head, "not another word, I'm sorry for touching you like that."

She reached up and kissed me hard on the mouth. "I want you to touch me too," she breathed against my mouth.

"I ..." I began, and this time she traced my mouth with her finger tips.

"Not today, but some time," she repeated. We both laughed out loud and came apart.

We spent the rest of the day walking over the dunes, her hand clinging wetly to mine. She racing suddenly down to the water, throwing off her sandals and running into the strong waves. I stood watching as she teased me to follow. I walked along the shoreline and had to run through the water to stay parallel, her jeans damp and dripping as she trotted onto the sand. I jogged back to get her towel, with her balancing on my shoulder to dry her feet. I was conscious of her closeness. Away again to explore the wired-off field. Helping her over the fence and making for the two rocks standing upright on a mound. Wondering if they were brought there in the olden days as a landmark for the trawlers. Thick sops of long grass grew nearby. She reached down to touch it saying, "Wouldn't this be a lovely place to catch the sun?" I smiled down on her. "Nobody ever comes up here either, and look at the view." I could see across to the Point, along the blue length of the river. The slight hills of Valentia running wild between the Atlantic and the sky. Backdrop to the New World. Wasteland of the emigrant young. My eyes were full of images, my mind struggling for the sky. "Dreamer," she was at my side again.

"Dream," I said touching her cheek lightly. She laughed and said, "I am so." I smiled and took her hand to walk down to the end of the field. No fence, just rocks and the sea brought the land to a stop. We hopped back along the rocks to the Strand.

The car was starting up for home. Only the solitary sand castle remained of the child. We talked of returning to the field of the green and long grass. We collected our bags and headed for home, stopping on the bridge to watch Mary's brother make a haul of salmon. Silver water fell to silence as the fish twitched in the nets on the Strand. The circular waves from the punt's path came to shore smaller and smaller. A time of evening that I loved to be on the bridge. Soft sun on the river. Ebb tide of evening. Tea-time in the town. The very day at rest. My silence answered by her face in repose. Reflected in still water and acknowledged by the sky. We said goodbye at the grotto and I watched her cycle up to her home. She moved a blue arm from her doorway, the evening sun warming her small smile as she entered. I pedalled home, off the saddle and half off the globe with dreams.

Chapter Twenty Three

My father at the table laying down the law about the bog. My mother setting out the salad in the scullery. Patches playing football out in the front with a boy from up town, his hair put on fire by the sun. "The turf's ready on the road for the lorry." My father telling my mother about hiring a lorry for Friday evening. I said I was playing soccer at seven. "What time are you going up?" I asked. "Six or seven, never mind the soccer."

"What's going to keep you warm in the winter?" he asked. No answer from me, staring into my cup. My mother taking the strain. "Ah boy, we never died a winter yet." He draining his tea, slapping his cap onto his head. Ancient winters had hardened him. In his time there was no boyhood. No question asked itself of him. Que sera sera, whatever will be, will be. His final resignation when the bitter wind rent the roof of the young Republic. The war years in London that my mother mentioned once to me. He working on the building, living in Cricklewood. She never knew him before London. Passing time in a watch factory. Serf of the Republic to the royal English. Laying their tables, scrubbing their spotless floors. Going to Mass on Sunday. Never losing her faith. Homesick for Derrymore, a handful of houses in a hill. Going to dances in the Galtymore on Sunday nights. Derrymore, Galtymore nominal home to thousands ... My father too, meeting on a London dance floor. Air raid shelter and cold darkness.

Hitler's black stars burning the London sky. "Only for that man Hitler ..." she said as she finished but she said no more. The crack was good in Cricklewood. He wanted to go back. I could see it in his eyes when our relations came home on holiday. Sitting forward to hear again the familiar names, Camden Town, Kilburn, Cricklewood, Paddington. I hated the

147

very sound of Paddington and I couldn't tell why. The crack ...
The past forever in my father's eyes.

He turned at the door. "Make it your business to be on the
lorry on Friday." He waited a while for an answer. The door
closed coldly and I looked up to find my mother's eyes warning
me. "Keep the peace for one evening. You can play the soccer
to your heart's content for the rest of the holidays." I smiled at
the way she said, "the soccer" as if it was a flagelette.

"Mam I want to tell you something," I pushed my cup away.

"What's troubling you lad," she said reaching for the teapot
on the range. I paused while she poured a cup. Sitting on my
father's chair opposite me she said, "Well?"

"The holidays you mentioned are my last," I said stirring my
tea. "I'm not going back to school." I looked up and saw the
sorrow furrowed to her brow. Her soft brown eyes seemed to
pale. Her heavy voice held her disappointment.

"You too." The Latin "et tu" echoed under my breath in
answer. "Brute," the name for betrayal. She asked me why and I
mumbled, "my eyes." Leaning forward on the table, earnestly
telling me about "throwing away a good education." The
chance to be clean instead of digging ditches. Finally the
coldest station in life, emigrant England.

The sun shining on the back window. The breeze lifting the
hem of the curtain in the front. A warm tea inside me. The
comfort of her calm before me and all round the eternal hills of
home. I listened and shrugged her words off the evening.

Friday, eve of Mid-Summer's day. Helping my mother clean
out the turf shed for the lorry. Opening the back gate wide; the
turf would be tipped in there. Filling a basket of broken white
sods to give for the bonfire. Sitting in the armchair, late in the
day, with my mother. She went in to answer a knock on the
front door. "Two soccer players at the door for you," she called
from the hall. I smiling to the door to greet them. Imploring me
to play against New Street. I telling them we were drawing the
turf home. Arguing with them, with myself ... Making a
promise that I'd do my best to be there. Closing the door on
their uncertain faces. My mother asking what they wanted.
Telling her earnestly that they were depending on me. "Your

own are depending on you too," she said. "The stranger can be second."

"They're my friends," I said without conviction.

"Make your own choice tomorrow. You're dressing a hard bed for yourself. Your father will want an early tea. I'd better go in. Don't forget to bring in the chair with you," she dragged her own chair up the back door steps. I lay deep in the armchair, closing my eyes on the sun.

The call from the scullery window. My mind divided throughout my tea. Patches spilling his cup in his excitement. Getting me to take down the clock from the mantlepiece, to set the alarm for the drawing in of the turf in the morning. Six o'clock. The Angelus bell ringing out. I walking out of the front door. No word from my mother. Strolling down the Marian and along to the bridge. Passing a quiet half-hour alone, looking at the play of sun on the water. The salmon boat under an arch waiting for a jump. A flash of dripping silver and the boat put out. Rowing beyond the disturbed water. The oars squeaking in rhythm to the straining arms of the two oarsmen. Helping to haul in the nets and getting splashed by the inwashing waves. Empty when the final strain was hauled to the strand. Mary's brother thanking me with a disappointed smile. I went up the steps by the end of the bridge as sorry as if it was my own failure. I watched them make one more haul willing the nets to be bloated; just a handful of small fish, pollock and bass I thought, were thrown up by the trawl. Nobody on the road as I walked back along Quay Street. Only a black donkey cropping the grass by the side of the small Terret. Climbing the Big Terret by the path generations of schoolboys dreaded and conquered. Looking back ... and smiling at my former fear. Resting on the rock where I first kissed Anna. Chewing on the stem of a bluebell. Watching the trawlers sail home, one by one. The fall out of the wash rippling the still shoreline. When calm returned to the river I got up to go. Over the wall of Bawnies and looking down on a lone boy dribbling a red rubber ball around two sticks; the goalposts. I stood on the top of the height admiring the balance of his body; he was scarcely six years old. The height making me run down to the cluster of cowslips that made the sideline of the pitch. The boy stopped and called out to me cheekily, challenging me to a game. I laughed and asked him how old did he think he was. "I'm six years and a bit, I can't stand here talking all day to you. Come on," and he passed the ball to me with the inside of his foot. I was eleven before I started kicking a ball properly. I shaped off a bit, juggling the ball before pushing it back to him. He imitated every trick I tried. He asked me if I was the best soccer player in town. I laughed and told him he was. He said I were silly. He wasn't. His witty way with words made me forget my decision and I was sorry when the other boys started to arrive. Some of the New Street boys stole his ball and went off over to the other goal.I was talking to the two Marian players who called for me earlier. He tugged at my elbow. "Will you get my ball back for me?" he looked up with his big brown eyes close to crying. I remembered how I first saw him, a boy and a ball; a part of his dream. To be the best soccer player in town. Small wish, his dearest for the time being. His life was made of moments, and his time was precious too. I told him not to worry and with my temper rising walked across the field. I didn't even have to open my mouth; the Sergeant's son gave me a kick. Bending down I scooped up the ball in my hands. "Handball," someone shouted. "Hands off!" was all I answered and turned my back. Not one word followed me as I made my way back to the boy. He thanked me and told me that I could play soccer with him anytime. "Anytime in the world," he repeated seriously and ran off solo-ing the ball. I missed him; he reminded me of someone, Patches maybe or ... I didn't know. A certain shadow had fallen when he turned his back. A singular shade of night had drawn. Across the sun a cloud called. A cold wind from the hills stirred. A memory ... The field was filling, down the road the chanting fell. From the Marian rival groups gathered to cheer. Standing on the fringe as the team was picked. Half hoping they wouldn't play me. I heard a lorry in the distance and knew it was too late. I thought it was going to stop outside the field but it only slowed for the bend. I hid behind the Sergeant's son who'd come across to spy. Watching the lorry disappear by the old graveyard tower. A red head stuck between the rails.

Patches in his element, hoping his friends would see him.

The ball on centre, New Street to kick off. Time over run, the game going against us. Playing by hurried instinct. New Street with their football boots and jerseys getting to grips with the ground. The assorted colours of the Marian in running confusion. Their team work told in the end. Scoring three to the goal I headed in consolation at the end. The evening was still stretching out when I stole away. Sweat was standing on my forehead, my shirt was clinging to my body. My mouth ached for water, my mind for mercy. The turf was home. I saw the black heap from the bathroom window. Patches tidying the sides that fell into the back garden. The lorry gone; my father taking the men up for a pint. I quenched my thirst from the cold water tap. Splashed my burning face until my eyes cooled. Saw the sun die, leaving it's remains on the far shore. A dark hint of gold left on the window. Black night arriving without illusions.

I turned to go; heard a footstep on the stairs that stopped me. I thought it was my mother and went to lock the door. I got to the sink when I saw it was my father. I couldn't close the door in his face. I pretended to wash my hands, turning the hot tap on. His face shadowed across the landing His urgent step and deliberate silence didn't prepare me. His fists across my face. The madness of the moon shining from his eyes. I crying out, inarticulate sounds making silence unreal. Pushed back against the wall, between the toilet and the hot press. Raising my hand to protect my face. Hearing words come from the darkness of his mouth. "Teach you … boy … do as … you're told, why?" The hardness of his fist punching my chest, landing with frightening force on my shoulders. My terrified mind wanted to fight back. I clenched my right hand to hit out at him. I couldn't hit him. I wanted to but I couldn't bring myself to act. I was nearly crying with fright; he wouldn't stop. Dimly I hear my mother, her two hands around his raised arm. I cowered in the corner for an instant, then burst past him into their bedroom, banging the door shut, louder than my heart. Hearing her come after me. Pressing my hands against the handle, my heaving chest against the frame. He twisted the handle in my hand; the door was coming in. It was then I thought he wanted to kill me.

His strength made matchwood of the door. I was pushed back as the door shoved open. The fear of death shook the foundation of my life. I looked to the window for escape. The thought of the concrete shattered me. The door was easing, my mother's back standing between him and me. It was the first time in my life I saw him raise his hand to her. After forever he went away. The door was pulled shut. My mother followed. I leaned weakly against the door. Smelling the paint he and I brushed together. All I could hear was the hammer of my heart. All I could see was the film of fear before my eyes. All I felt was the hardness of his hands. All I could remember was the distant days we would never share again. All I ... As near to total loss in that dark room as I would ever be in my life. Something grew hard in me. Out of the pain in my body a suffering silence took hold. My father never saw a smile in my eyes again. He never heard me speak without a word from him first. I watched him suffer. The partition of pride held; only death could bring the border down. I often thought it was like Ireland's ancient injustice: the child's vision of a broken world. I was forever Ireland, always adolescent. Realizing I was wrong too late. Ten years. Too late to know my father's forgiveness. The house was quiet when I left the room. Only the running sound of the water from the tap, still turned on. I washed my face and hands. Went to the window; it was dark outside. Patches still bent to his task. The hill had lost the last scattering of sunset.

I stepped slowly downstairs; past the kitchen door and into the night. Out of the corner of my eyes I saw my mother behind the open curtain. Her eyes watching me walk away. What sorrow did they hold? Alone in the empty kitchen. Not even the glow of a winter fire for company. I could almost picture her going to the range to stir the cold ashes for something to do tonight. He would have gone back up town. I hoped I wouldn't meet him. The night air cooled my face as I passed up by the old tower. My arms were cold and I remembered I only had a tee-shirt on. I inhaled the rural air; smell of hay and heather, dung and dust. My eyes still blind, at home in the shadows. My mind festering with stricken feelings. Making my way back town; I passed the Sergeant's son. I said "hello," and left him standing in his doorway looking after me, for once lost for a word. Out Valentia Road, flitting silently by the night walkers. Half built house on the left, and beyond a meadow the red roof of Guard Murray's where once I cut my knee on the gravel front. Small hurt remembered as I walked towards the only light ahead; two houses by a brook. Silent water flowing softly seaward. Up the height to the Obs. listening to a corncrake inside the ditch. Hayfields running down to the old railway tracks; a field of friesian cows above the road, and me breaking the stillness with my aimless step. I turned back at the Obs. facing home again. My country under night. My town lending me light. My house at the end of the road. All unknown; strange places in my mind. Another leaving, not of the world of ten, was the answer. I would go away, find a job in Dublin or … I didn't know, without even the Inter what papers did I have? The Primary proving I could read and write and reckon. I was trapped.

The light was on when I turned into the square. I went straight upstairs to my room. Patches was asleep, face to the wall, a hand thrown away from him across the sheet. I undressed quickly, expecting a call from below. No call came and I lifted Patches's hand and gently placed it by his side. He half stirred but didn't wake up. I slipped in beside him and lay on my back. For a long time I gazed at the ceiling with my eyes wide open. I slept without ever remembering closing my eyes.

Chapter Twenty Four

Morning. Awakening. Early by the silence at my window. The
bed clothes on the floor. My bare shoulders ached with cold
and pain. My mind with remembrance. Behind the curtain the
room was light. Patches was curled like a ball in the middle of
the bed. I tried to sleep again, pulling the bedclothes from the
floor and up over my head. A woman's sharp heel on the
concrete. Voices of children out in the front. A dog barking
and a man shouting, "go to bed." The kitchen door opening,
listening for my mother's step on the stairs. Too aware of the
living light to sleep. The door closing again; my mother having
taken the milk from under the stairs. The "cool" she called it,
her fridge in the hot summer months. The day was filling with
sounds. I raised myself on my elbow, looking for my clothes.
They were thrown across the brown chair by the bed. I got out
and slipped yesterday's tee-shirt over my head. Going to the
window to see what kind of day was out. Blue sky to celebrate
the twenty-first of June. The sun's longest journey to set
beneath the evening. Mid-summer morning, bonfire night …

Washing in the bathroom, looking out over the shallow river
to the twin hills. Two shadows as yet unclaimed by the sun.
Felt the loneliness of the land. Took in the black heap of turf
and decided I would draw it into the shed without my mother
asking. Ashes in the air, my mother bending over the range,
lighting the fire. Telling me to open the back door without
looking around at me. The air enticing the ashes from the
kitchen. I took a bowl from the scullery shelf and found the
cornflakes on the table. My mother, finished with the fire,
making a fresh pot of tea. Gentle banter about the bog to bring
out the first smile. Telling her I lost the game along with
everything else. She sitting down to have a cup with me. A

certain sadness crossing her eyes when she looked to the window. "Expecting a letter from London," she said. "Are you expecting any line yourself lad?" she had a way of making her voice sound earnest in fun.

I answered, "I'm not fishing this weather," and she laughed out loud. I didn't think it was that funny but joined her smile anyway.

After breakfast I found an old pair of shoes with a bit of twine for laces. My mother teasing that I looked like Con the Laces, an old traveller out of my childhood. I faintly remembered seeing him shuffling from door to door. A shabby black coat tightened around him by a length of string. Selling fine laces while his own shoes held yellow cord. He left the pain of many question marks in my eyes when I watched him pass my door. Pass my door to get past my life. He died and I missed him most in the spring, his time for visiting. Another swallow on the skyline. I heard he died in a ditch by the side of a road. I believed the swallows took him home with them when they left for the warm world in the autumn. I had read about the legend of the young boy who waited at the gable of his father's cottage to welcome the swallows to Ireland. He was called Oweneen of the Swallows. When they gathered one evening the boy knew the spring was on the land and every evening they would rest on a nearby tree. Welcomed and watched over by the lonely boy who had no brothers or sisters. Until one evening when they never returned to the tree. The boy waiting until the cold night had settled over the empty, empty sky. Looking for the last time to the west for a sign. The swallows had gone away to the warm world, leaving autumn behind. The grass, the flowers, the leaves would all fade. Everything would die in the absence of the swallows. Everything but the limpid loneliness in a boy's eyes. When you're six even the swallows have a measure of meaning. Now, with my old shoes tied by string an old man had an epitaph written in my memory. Under the constitution Con the Laces was never a child. To think a child of six could treasure a season of swallows more than a nation could treasure a man. I could see it was unfair to blame the nation for the man but could I forget a man called Con the

Laces.

The postman passing the window as I made for the back door. My mother following me out, to go upstairs to call Patches. Saying, "no letter, no line, no parcel, no news from the road" to me as she stepped heavily on the stairs. I hadn't seen her read a letter by the back window for an age. Someone was lost in London ... The cold morning air shielded from the sun by houses. A shadow of smoke from the chimney linked the late potato stalks. The end of the garden was bordered by the sun. Reaching over the house tops, angling from the east. The garden gate was off the hinges. Most of the turf lay scattered where it was tipped in the passageway. Getting the turf pike from the shed I stood resting my arms on it like the County Council workers would. They were well known for their hard contemplation. I smiled at my posture, a joke coming into my mind. A young boy up in a plane asking his father what the tiny dots down on earth were. The father answering "if they move the're cattle, if they don't move the're County Council men."

I started rooting at the turf with the pike but the heap was too tightly packed. Finding the old wheelbarrow I filled it by hand. The children started to arrive with their offers of help. Whenever a house was drawing in the turf a gather of kids would occur. I let them all at it; some of the younger ones barely able to lift a sod without the whitening of both hands. Patches put in an appearance, wiping away a yawn with his arm. Without lifting a finger he issued orders left, right and centre. The morning wore on. Sweat mounting on my forehead. Stopped for milk and water and a few minutes survey. My mother came out to help and I went in the shed to tidy and clamp the turf. By half-eleven there was only the few half sods left in the passage. My mother gave me some change to pay the children. Two shillings to one, sixpence to another and a consolation of coppers to the young ones. They all trooped away happily shouting promises to be back again next year. My mother sighed, "talk of element. I've a pain in the head from listening to them."

I cleared up alone. Patches was in the kitchen with my

mother demanding a half-crown for his labours. I went into the cool of the house. Washed the sweat from my face. Shook the turf dust from my hair. Changed into my other tee shirt and put my sand shoes on. Caught my reflection on the wardrobe mirror: all blue like Anna was that day in the White Strand. I walked up for the *Press*. The tar was melting on the road. I met the young boy kicking the red rubber ball against the green garage. He stopped and asked me about the game, scratching his head in disbelief when I said, we lost 3-1. "Who got the goal? You?" he questioned further. "I did," I smiled. "I thought you might, did you header it?" I laughed at his expectant expression. "It was a simple goal," I laughed again. "But it takes a simple man to score a simple goal," he grinned cheekily. I made to cuff his ear in fun and he ducked away to dribble the ball and give a commentary as he ran. "Pele on the ball now." Pele! The black beauty in every boy who'd kick a ball.

Dom was cutting a countryman's sparse hair and I took the paper from a stand by the window. Our name was written across the top alongside "the truth in the news" motto. My mother referred to the *Irish Press* as Dev's Daily. I'd read an *Irish Independent* once. I didn't like the way it was laid out; all the news cluttered up. I heard two Leaving Cert boys argue about the two papers one day. The boy defending the *Independent*, getting exasperated and saying hotly, "Jesus, it's true what they say, love is blind." That was alluding to De Valera's eyesight and the other boy got a bit political over the remark. I turned to the back page when I gained the door. I had the habit of reading the sports pages first. Back to front like Chinese writing.

My mother was putting the dinner on the plates when I got back. The radio was on, playing Irish music. There was a programme on every Saturday which ended with the announcer saying, "and if you feel like singing do sing an Irish song." I used to say "don't" to drown his "do" and my mother would chide me. My head was still in the paper when my father came in.

"Come on, come on, throw it out," he said as usual, taking

157

his cap off and going to his place at the table. I didn't raise my head when he asked, "is the turf in yet?" He was pleased when my mother told him "long 'go this morning; we're the servants for you."

My mother called for dinner and I said I'd eat later. I didn't want to sit at the same table as him. He knew it. I heard him say, "If he was hungry, he'd ate." I made no reply just turned a page indifferently. My mother tried to include me in the talk from the table. I only answered her. The pips for the news went at half-one. He said, "turn the radio up." I didn't stir and my mother got up to raise the volume. The rule of silence for the news was welcome for once. At a quarter to he put his cap on to go back to work. I sat down to my dinner while my mother was drinking her tea. We always had tea after dinner. My father liked it strong and you could nearly eat it by the time I was ready for my cup. I listened to the sponsored programmes until three o'clock; Radio Eireann went off the air them. I heard a song called, "Halfway to Paradise," that I liked. It was sad, soft. Better than the bitter hymns to the Blessed Virgin Eire. How could I love something that called me to hate. The border, the British ... "All that delirium of the brave." I refused the call. The glorious calendar of 1916 still hanging on green walls could be taken down. The ban on foreign games fostered in the Kingdom of Kerry by men who pledged allegiance to the Kingdom of God, that embraced all men. The compulsory Irish that could make all other subjects null and void if you failed it. The fawning fear of the clerical frown that furrowed the country more deeply than any plough. Any star...born to follow or unfurl. I thought about these things now, questioning every law of man and God's supremacy in the firmament of Ireland. Picking up the *Press* again I dragged an armchair out the back. The day deepened and I half-read, half-thought...dozed off in the warm shadow of the wall that reduced the sun to softness.

It was tea-time; my mother calling me out of my dreams. I opened my eyes and felt my forehead. It was warm and gold with the sun on my fringe. I picked up the fallen paper and lifted the armchair in the back steps. The cool of the house washed over me. Splashing cold water over my face in the bathroom. Out the window I could see the site of the bonfire. Turf and green trees, tyres and timber. The river looked dazed and low. The twin hills waited to receive the declining sun.

Early tea; young lettuce, spring onions, triangles of Galtee cheese, beetroot and fresh ham. The shop bread still warm from the bakery, causing the butter to run. A pound pot of raspberry jam in the shade by the window. The teapot drawing on the range. My mother pulling the back curtains to keep the sun off the butter. Pouring out the first cup to Patches. Finally sitting in my father's place under the picture of the Mother of Perpetual Succour. I liked this time of evening with nothing outside to draw me. The town indoors except for the young children, innocent of time. Out the front window I could see the sun splashed on the upstairs window of the house opposite. I took in the grass in shadow and the grass lit green by the free light. The contrast divided by the narrow white concrete. The only sound was Patches trying to get an extension of his usual time to be in. My mother trying to make it an hour this side of midnight and Patches trying for the small hours. Eventually they compromised on midnight. I remained quiet, wondering would Anna be out tonight. Drawn to the fire, the music in the square, the restless night. Who would stay behind the curtain; even my mother would rise out tonight.

Patches gulped his second cup and dashed out for fear he'd miss any excitement. His red hair blazed past the window. The house fell silent. "He's mad for road," my mother shook her head, gathering up his cleaned plate and cup. I poured another cup of tea, my third and pondered alone in the alcove. The clock ticking on the mantelpiece. My mother humming in the scullery. A distant bee buzzing. Small sounds of summer. The Angelus announcing the night. My mother fell silent in the scullery. A time for prayer…peace. I finished my tea as my father was getting off the bike outside the window. Carefully throwing his leg out over the carrier.

I ducked out the front while he was putting the bike under the stairs. I leaned against the porch, inhaling the evening air. Smell of burning rubber, exploding carbon and the deep smoke from the chimneys. It was still quiet in the square; only a few boys putting matches to golden syrup tins filled with carbon. More often than not the lid would fall flat instead of shooting off for a distance. The fire wouldn't be lit for another hour at least. I decided to stay awhile before going down to give a hand to build it.

The fishermen passed up, walking awkwardly in their long white rubbers. Unhurried. One modest salmon, shimmering even in death. Mary's brother carried a bag tied in half with a throng of thick rope. I knew that it was filled with pollock and bass. Only the salmon would be carried with pride. The children would run up to the fishermen and Mary's brother would give an estimate of their weight that the scales would always support. As my mother would say "he was an expert man." During the off season he ferried tourists to the Skellig Rock. I watched the fishermen disappear around the bend at Bawnies Field.

Chapter Twenty Five

A few people were going up to meet the bus. A homecoming of a son or daughter. Carrying the self-conscious case down the street. All eyes open for style and change, weight or want. I wondered if my sister would be coming home. A year come September she went away. The children from uptown were making their way down in droves to see which street had the biggest fire. The Rock, the Marian, East End's which was held in the Fair Field and the Camps down by the bridge. The Marian was best for music and the square was perfect for dancing. The men began to pass up, their working clothes discarded. White shirted and their faces shined with shaving. Most of them had dark suits with the trousers turned up. As my mother remarked when my father was buying a suit, "a white shirt and a navy suit is very dressy." It was the men's Sunday for receiving and the Saturday evening would be taken up with a hair-cut, confession and a pint. As I watched them go up I remembered I had to have a hair-cut myself. I went in; my mother was cutting a square of home-made bread in the scullery. I asked her for the price of the hair-cut and she took four shillings from behind the bread bin. I had a shilling change for myself. Hair-cuts had gone up sixpence since the last time I went. I ran up to my room to comb my hair before setting out for Dom's. I gave a quick glance to Anna's house; her sister who was one age with Patches jumped into view. I smiled to myself, thinking of the September evening I watched from my window; "all she wants is gold and silver, all she wants is a nice young man!"

The sun was warm on the back of my neck. Bawnies Field looked bare and burned, except on the height. Here the blades of long grass glinted as the light caught them. They'd be no football played tonight. I met nobody on the way. Dom was cutting a countryman's hair. Grey at the sides and matted on top by the peaked cap he wore. I said "hello" to Dom and sat on one of the waiting chairs. They were covered in red leather luxury. I listened to Dom and the farmer talking about fishing and football and the state of the country. The man bought a *Kerryman* on the way out, telling Dom "I'm only getting it for the care. Indeed there's more news in yourself Dom, for nothing! Good luck and thanks."

"For nothing," Dom replied winking at me behind the farmer's back. "And what can I do for you?" Dom said tucking the towel behind my neck. He always said that and I answered, "a hair-cut."

"A hair-cut indeed," he echoed. He asked me about the bonfire and who was going to have the biggest crowd for the crack. He was a great man for dancing. He went to all the socials in the wintertime: dinner dances and dos. I told him the Marian was the place to be tonight. I liked to just sit there with the smell of falling hair, the hair oil and the soothing powder he put on my neck at the end. His slow mellow voice making me drowsy as he talked. The clipping sound of the scissors the only edge on the otherwise silent evening. Even his hands were soft and clean as he angled my head to cut behind my ears. He used a hair cutter which he plugged in to cut the back. The cats-hairs on my neck hurt as the machine sometimes caught. I got on to talking soccer near the end. He was wondering how United would get on next season. We had hardly began when a GAA man walked in. That put paid to United. The talk turned to Gaelic after that and Dom brushed the hairs from my shoulders and rubbed hair oil on my hair. I paid the four shillings and he gave me sixpence change. "Good luck Dom," I called at the door and he answered, "goodbye now."

The back of my neck was cold and I itched as I ran down the road. Rounding the corner at Bawnies I saw the crowd gathering. Children were coming from all directions, some carrying last minute offerings, a branch, a bag and even a sod of turf. I put on a sprint to get in and brush my neck. All the doors were open, my father was in the kitchen polishing his shoes. I

162

passed straight upstairs and wiped my neck with a damp face cloth. I heard my father on the tiles in the hall. He'd be going up to confession. I left him go for a time and bounded down the stairs. My mother was at the kitchen door, "and what time are you going to be in tonight?" she asked. "Morning Missus," I answered airily. She called after me "I'll give you till two!"

"Alright so," I shouted back and ran to meet the oncoming night.

The Leaving Cert boys were sprinkling paraffin on the clamp of turf that formed the fire. Some were bundling old newspaper and stuffing it between the openings in the reek. A tractor tyre crowned the top and the broken turf was being fired in to the tyre. Finally all was set for the match. It took nearly a box of matches to get it fully blazing. Dark blue smoke smouldered under the warm sky. Cheers rent the air and children danced round the fire. I saw Patches chasing a boy from uptown, a thin boy with rimless glasses. The last time I saw them together they were disputing the colour of the moon. I wondered what the argument was this time. I helped the Sergeant's son keep the fire blazing. Even though he was from New Street he had influence. I piled on green branches cut from the old graveyard. All the turf was gone and only car tyres and logs remained. Very few parents ventured near. They'd arrive rapidly when the music livened up the night.

Anna's sister was out and she looked up at me with a knowing smile. I blushed and nodded at her. She went off laughing with her companion. I grabbed Patches as he charged after a gang of girls . He didn't know it was me and he gave me an elbow in the ribs. I pressed the sixpence in his hand and sent him up for sweets, when I recovered my breath. He wasn't over-anxious to please but I wouldn't let go until he promised. He got his pal from uptown to go with him and he raced off happily enough. The Sergeant's son and myself stretched out on the grass for a while. I listened to him go on about all the girls he shifted and whom he was going to try tonight. He had his eye on the newest banker's daughter. There were two of them; one fourteen and the other fifteen. I didn't know them only to see. It was enough. I saw them at communion, superior

163

types marching back, wiggling their hips as if He had received them. I let him talk; I couldn't stop him anyway. He was no great shakes but he had faith. Moves mounds as he himself said. I knew what he meant but didn't let on. Patches returned and I gave him two toffees. He'd lost his friend. The girls started to arrive, giggling and nudging. Summer frocks and white stocking up to their knees. Some hid their girlish legs in women's wear; tan nylons and high heels. Teetering on the brink of womanhood. The Sergeant's son got talking to three or four of them, flannelling them with flattery. He tried to drag me into the conversation but I only answered out of politeness. I felt quiet, the loud laughter breaking over me without touching.

I got up and looked westward. The evening had stretched out. The sun scattered on the horizon. Hovering above before sinking out of sight. Leaving the remnants of red on the skyline. I felt a restlessness sweep over me. There was no sign of Anna. The curtains were drawn on her window. She never said whether she'd be out tonight. I never asked specific time of her. It was understood, like Mass on Sunday. The square was filling up; I thought I heard a melodeon being opened and squeezed. I wondered what time it was; turned to ask the Sergeant's son but he had vanished. He might have said, I thought. Perhaps he did and I heedless with my own thoughts. I picked my way thro' the throng of people. As I got closer to the square the music started up. Jigs or reels or racket. I couldn't abide it whatever it was called. I was a minority of one. Wild yahoos shook the sky. Shouts of "good on yourself" and "that's the crack." The countrymen were in town.

My mother was standing in the door. "What's the time Mam?" I called from the gate. "Nine o'clock lad, time for any white boy to be in bed."

"With this ding-dong." I walked up to the step. "Isn't it glorious music." she kidded me. I made a face and she laughed. The woman next door came along and they strolled down to the square. My mother had left a bottle of coke on the table for me. There was a plate of biscuits out too. I took a few Mikado and custard creams. Patches liked the Kimberley but I could take them or leave them. I left them.

Sitting on the sofa, a chair drawn up to act as table for the snack. Wondering whether to go to bed, take the radio up with me. On impulse getting up, switching it on and turning the dial away from Radio Eireann to Lux. A request was being read out in a light American accent. "Are You Lonesome Tonight." A request......a reality. I listened and quenched my thirst on "the real thing." I thought of my sister in London and how she sang another Elvis song, "Wooden Heart." The radio started crackling and I switched off.

The music from the square welled up into the night. I could hear the men pound the concrete, emphasising the end of a set. Shouts of encouragement from those sitting out the dance and the tinkle of the women's laughter as they were swung in a wild waltz. I could never picture myself out there on the square. Before the night was out my father would be stepping it out. One night in memory of olden times at a crossroads of another summer's evening. I'd be embarrassed for him and more for my mother if she was drawn into the wild whirling. Switching the kitchen light off I went to the front door for one last look. The lilting loveliness of the "Rose of Tralee" wafted on the summer breeze.

"The pale moon was rising above the green mountain,
the sun was declining beneath the blue sea,
As I strayed with my love neath the clear crystal fountain
that stands in the beautiful vale of Tralee."

It was light outside. Pale stars scattered around a crescent moon. The blue of the day had held to the night sky. The white light from the moon shone on the concrete square giving it an appearance of softness. The dancing couples looked like wraiths from a puppet pageant. Invisible strings were tugging at my will. Trying to pull me out under the naked light. To make me give expression to the absolute unity of the people out there, my own. I stood fast to the shadows. The ancient music, too lively tonight for thought, only reached my ears, while I knew it could touch the atavistic soul of my father as it moved generations. And I , alone, like a stag poised for flight across

165

the mountain. No silver streams at evening. No sudden silence in a blue morning. No rest at any clearing. A kingdom of pride and loneliness. I.

The music stopped, briefly. Another player was taking over. My father's favourite song saddened the summer silence.

"Alone all alone on a wave washed strand,
And alone in a crowded hall,
The hall it is gay and the waves they are grand,
But my heart is not here at all."

For the first time I noticed the light was switched on on the ESB pole. People were milling about laughing and chatting. The women drawing discarded cardigans round their shoulders while they waited to be asked out in a set. In the interlude I crept out like an interloper. Standing on the verge of the crowd, looking for my mother or Patches. Even the face of my father...looking for someone.

"It flies far away by night and by day,
To the times and the joys that are gone,
But I never will forget the sweet maiden I met,
In the valley of Slievenamon."

I glanced down towards the fire; it was still blazing. The younger children had it all to themselves now. Some were struggling to feed the flames. Others overcome with the excitement and the late hour sat on the warmed grass, quietly gazing into the heart of the fire. Fighting to stay awake and fascinated by the shooting arrows from the flames. A dance was called and the couples formed a circle. When they broke I saw my sister dancing with a course-faced country boy. He lived up towards Carhan and I knew him to nod to. I didn't see my father or my mother and I was relieved. Towards the climax of the dance the men had to swing the women. As my sister swirled to a stop the boy swung her off her feet and crushed her against his chest. I turned away hoping nobody would notice the embarrassment burning my face. I walked out to the empty road. I saw the Sergeant's son get off with the banker's eldest daughter. She going in the gate of Bawnies while he vaulted the wire fence. The dark rocks of the Big Terret or the flat top of Bawnies, I knew, that's where I wanted to be tonight; Anna knew. I kept wandering, now and then getting inside the crowd. Warm and flushed the women set their perfume on the air, mingling with the smell of hay and hill. The shallow sound of the sea could be heard in the silence between tunes. The tide breaking on the shore with the regular roll of the gravel. Hollow night.

> "By night and by day, I ever ever pray,
> While lonely my life flows on,
> To see our flag unroll and my true love to enfold,
> In the valley of Slievenamon."

Chapter Twenty Six

"Hello," so softly she said it that I turned the other way first. Anna was tugging at my sleeve, at my racing heart. Turning again I said, "Hello," and searched for words to keep her. Her face shone white in the moonlight. Her eyes darkened by the shadow thrown by her cascading hair. I smelt the shampoo; she must have stayed in to wash it tonight. Strands of hair glinted as she raised her head for the moonlight to wash over it. Showering her hair with pale gold. My stomach turned over as a shy smile played about her lips. My own lips were frozen; I felt a nerve twitch in my face. I couldn't take my eyes from her curved face. I wanted to hold her, in darkness and in silence and in love.

Anna spoke first, alluding to the music and dancing. "There's great excitement here tonight,"

I shrugged indifferently, "nothing to write home about." She looked surprised at my tone and said "You don't like things Irish?"

"I do," I put pain in my voice. "I like you," and I smiled for the first time tonight.

"Oh you" was all she answered, digging her small fist into my ribs. "Well I want to watch anyway." She moved a step towards the ring around the dancing. She paused and invited me with a word, "coming?" I followed, dragging my heels, looking to see if anyone's eyes were on me. She had charmed her way past a group of old countrymen and I slipped thro' the crack in the crowd after her. I was standing behind her looking over her shoulder. A white-haired old man dancing a jig. I watched her face in profile, a half-smile dancing on her lips. When the music ended she caught me looking. As she swung her head the light from the ESB pole found the smile in her eyes. I felt myself

168

smiling sillily back at her. The music started up again and the crowd closed pushing me up behind her. The warm outline of her body pressed into me and a shock of softness went through me. I raised my hands but didn't know what to do with them. Alone I would place them on her shoulders. I looked round, feeling stupid with my hands raised like surrender. Lightly I brought them down on her shoulders. She started a little but edged backwards into the crook of my arms. I was now hoping the music would go on all night. Play for ever so I could hold her and taste the soft perfume of her hair.

A burden had left my back. Leaving school seemed like wilful waste. My eyes had a new light tonight. I could even face wearing glasses now. My life would change, my self-bred loneliness would be no more. The wonder of the world would give back my faith. The wistfulness of her eyes would mirror my dreams and if they were sad in September, what matter. She would walk by me. Silent, maybe, when speaking was uncalled for. When the fields were black at five. The hills white with mist. The river swollen with relentless rain and my pen scratching away the winter night. Alone in my room with only Pythagorus and Virgil for company and her face at my window when I pulled the curtain on the deep and dark night. Gazing into the black world; the cold wind whipping the grass to the ground. Away in the distance the sound of cattle bellowing, sheltering against a dreary ditch. A coldness coming over me. A winter wasteland trying to find a home in my mind. Closing the curtain and stirring the last dying embers of the fire. Picking up Virgil's Aeneid, flicking the pages. Thinking of her and my own journey. Settling down to do my homework diligently; to apply the Latin adverb. To get the Leaving, honours, a clean job in Dublin. Collar and tie. Mass on Sunday. My personal pride and my precious soul saved. The music had stopped. The dancers drifted apart. The women and girls clustering to one side, claiming cardigans to keep warm. The men standing awkwardly, lighting cigarettes. The crowd shifted and shuffled about us. My arms were still resting on her shoulders. She was turning in my hands. I was waiting, letting her shoulders slide around until her full face was close to mine. Her eyes were quiet, shaded by her fallen lashes. I lifted her chin with the palm of my hand. Her eyes gazed silently up at me. "Come for a walk," was all I uttered knowing there was everything to be said tonight.

Shouldering a way thro' the crowd, leading her away. Beyond the shelter of the people the air had turned chilly. She half ran to keep up with me, her unbuttoned cardigan slipping off her shoulders. I paused and without speaking wrapped it to her slenderness. She thanked me in a child-like voice, breathless and broken. I had no place in mind as we walked down towards the fire. The foundation of the fire was still sound. The flames had died down; the tyres had burned out. I stopped for a short while feeling the solid heat sting my sunburned face. I walked on, leaving the sleepy children behind. Soon a distance and a darkness had parted us from the people. The music was fading with every step. We walked down the road by the grotto. I always knew it by "the road." No name, leading to the pier and on to the bottom of Railway Street towards the bridge.

I drew her towards me for the first time under the black shadow of the Big Terret. Stopping silently and finding her lips in the darkness. We kissed for a long time, awkwardly, saying nothing to each other. Only the low tide taking to the far shore disturbed the night. Now and then a corncrake sundered the silence with its rusty croak. We walked on, her cool hand slipping into mine. I was thinking of the future I foresaw while the music played. Her body resting in my arms and my life held in my own hands. Thinking of the bridge before me.

She talked a little as we strolled along. About the summer turning. The tourists returning to England and America. After the regatta only the races to look forward to. Then back to school to prepare for the Inter. Her voice filling the still night like soft summer rain. By the small Terret I stopped to look down on the dock. I could only see the square of shelter where the small punts and motor boats were moored. The moon sailing giddy across the river. Under the light the water was silk and silent, even sacred for a moment. She moved close to me, her shoulder touched my chest. I released her hand and put an arm around her shoulder. Something touched her too. I asked her what was the matter. Her eyes were wide on the river, pools of pain in the light.

She held her tongue for a time before telling me she was thinking of the Valentia boy. His graveyard in the deep. The night of the fallen star. Her brother.

I turned her from the river with my arm, "come away." She looked up and smilingly added "O human child." I squeezed her to me and teased, "some child." She laughed lightly and replied, "some faery." Laughing loudly, together we walked under the shadow of the small Terret. Slowly, without talking, holding close. The smell of furze, of fuchsia, of ferns, gave scent to a slight chill in the air. The warmed earth smelled of green grass gone to gold. Bleached and burned like the after-grass of a meadow. Out of the shadows the road was lit by the ESB pole near the entrance to the old railway station. To the right the convent and the Daniel O'Connell Hotel dominated the buildings along Railway Street, blotting out the left shoulder of Beenatee. The Kingdom Cinema opposite was puny by comparison. I thought how great it would be on a Saturday night in the depths of winter to take her to the pictures.

We passed the old railway station where I used to go to meet my relations in the summer. I loved that crowded platform with everybody gazing across the length of the river to the black railway bridge. It was there that the first glimpse of smoke would be sighted. Then the homeward hoot and the engine would nose into view. The sun striking the shining black funnel. The windows open and filled with pale white city faces.

When the line closed that part of town died. Now people had to go up town to meet the bus, outside the dance hall. It was not the same. All that remained of the railway was the roofless walls of the waiting room and the solitary sign on the notice board. All that would remain of the railway in years to come would be the name of the street.

"Look at Alma Mater," she was saying. "What does it remind you of?"

"A perfect prison," I said with feeling.

"Ah it's not that bad," she laughed. "Is it so bad at the Brothers?"

"It was, past tense," I replied.

"Why, you're not leaving surely?" she stopped walking in surprise.

"I'm not going back in September," I said evenly.

"Are you going away, to boarding school so?" she pursued standing in front of me.

"No," I replied. "I'm never going back to any school again."

"But why?" she raised her voice on the question.

"Oh, you know, if is the obstacle?"

She said, "Yes," doubtfully.

"Well, why is the fall," I said flatly.

She slapped my face lightly. "You're making a fool of me."

"I wish I was." I caught her hand and brought it back to my face.

She put her arms around my neck and I held her to me. "Well you can tell me," she broke free and her face was clouded with concern. I started walking and answered as she caught up.

"I'll tell when we find a place to sit down."

"The bridge?" she suggested.

"Too hard, the strand would be better," I replied.

We reached Quay Street, a huddle of small houses in an old part of town. At the other end was a water pump that supplied the street. A lot of old people seemed to live there. I often saw them drawing water in white enamel buckets. A man on a bike passed us and said, "goodnight." He turned over the bridge; ahead the old RIC barracks stood, overlooking the river. It was said there were guns buried there from the time of the Troubles. As we drew near I could make out the sucking sound of the whirlpools beneath the bridge. It made me shiver and she said, "Are you getting cold?" She moved closer as I nodded.

Our steps made an empty sound as we entered the bridge. Ahead the hill was buried on the other side of the moon. Black patches of cloud appeared above the horizon. The air was still except for a slight freshening from the river and always and endless the waves of water beating against the bridge. Something lonely in the sound of the sea. Of emptiness and futility and sometimes freedom. Hollow now with the shallow water grating on the gravel. On each of the solid supports there was a landing square and we made for the first one. Silently we both looked down on the whirling water. She spoke first. "It makes me shiver. Is it true that the whirlpools suck you down?"

I tried to make light of her remark. "Only if you fall in," I said serious.

"Oh you, why can't you be serious with me?" she shouldered me gently.

"I'm sorry." I hung my head. "It's my defence against fear," I added.

"What are you afraid of?" She leaned back against the bridge.

"The whirlpools, the future, but mostly the past," I said hurt by her distance. She remained silent, her face in shadow. The breeze from the night river blowing thro' the fenders and playing about the hem of her skirt. Now and then a sharp gust enticing it to rise.

Half her thighs showed, her skirt climbing and clinging. I tried to look away but my eyes were drown to a flash of whiteness. She quickly caught the hem and stooped to draw it down over her gleaming legs. I felt myself blush and was thankful for the night time. As she raised her face her eyes held mine. I was locked without decision for a moment. Another gust from the river raised the skirt. She made no attempt to cover her bare legs. Her head moved higher until she was level with my eyes. The whites narrowed and the pupils darkened. Her lips parted and her teeth glinted. I knew I was expected to make a move. I wanted, but I waited, holding her eyes and dropping my gaze to her thighs. The skirt was billowing up and down as the squalls took it. Finally her lips closed and tightened. She gave me a look and asked, "why are you afraid of me?" I looked from her face to her legs. Without waiting for my answer she reached down to her skirt. Without a word I clasped my hand over hers. She stopped tugging at her skirt and my hands were left alone on her cold thighs. I could feel the skimpy material ride down over my hands. I eased her back against the bridge moving my hands up under her skirt. I could feel the swell of her body against me. She made no effort to shake away my hands. I took one hand away and grasped her

173

waist as I reached down to find her lips. As we kissed I rubbed my hand up the back of her thighs, finding them warm as my hand reached to fondle the soft curve jutting from the elastic. Her breasts were taut against my chest and when I fumbled at the buttons of her blouse she tore her mouth from mine. My body was on fire and my voice was hoarse as I whispered, "Afraid of you now, am I afraid, am I?" I repeated.

"No, no you're not," she was crying as she pulled away against the railings. Her bottom banged against the concrete and a sharp pain shot my hand out from underneath her skirt. She caught my other hand at her breast and stopped me unbuttoning her blouse. She was still crying. "Not here, not here." She finally broke away leaving me shivering with excitement. We stood apart, strangers to one another. I wondered what had come over her to taunt me with her body. I asked her why and she said "Because you're so cool about things."

"What things?" I asked.

She answered instantly, "about sin and death and things."

"I don't know what you mean by that, but if you ask me there's only one great sin and that is to die, and neither you nor I can ever be absolved from that." My breathing was breaking the words up as I spoke.

She retorted hotly. "That's foolish talk, we must die to live forever."

"Well," I paused "touching you isn't going to end your everlasting life, is it?"

"It's an occasion of sin," she said shortly. "So is dancing," I said in the same tone. No reply came from her, she just half turned to look down on the rippling water. I watched her, holding my patience with an effort. I felt I was losing her. She was asking questions of me and I was not talking. I didn't know what to do, stop or go. Either way, I'd be alone. She turned from her reflection and said evenly.

"This river is an occasion of sin to you so."

"What!" I couldn't believe my ears. The Fertha! It's only a raindrop on the Atlantic."

"My brother drowned in that water. Wasn't that a mortal sin

by your way of wondering?" she spoke bitterly into my face. I turned cold. The night of nights returned to fall on me again. Black and bitter piercing the wound in my memory.

She was standing before me, her hands clasped for comfort round her waist. Her fringe ruffled and held back from her forehead by the wind. A little girl lost look about her face. Even her shoulders dropped to complete her resignation. I remained silent. How long had I held this silence? Could I be silent forever?

To buy time I touched her tense arm saying, "come on down to the strand." She made no move to follow and I committed myself to her pity. "Come on," I repeated, "and I'll show you where the greatest occasion occurred, and more, much more than I could ever say to anybody else." She was startled by my say and let her hands fall from her waist. Without a word escaping her open mouth she stepped off the column. Together we walked over the bridge, our steps sounding off the cold concrete. She never prompted me to speak. We walked apart. At the end of the bridge on the left, stone steps led down to the strand. A rusty turnstile had to be negotiated at the top. I was on the inside and led the way down. The strand was covered in faint darkness. The outline of the shore rippled. I trod carefully on the second step. She was standing above me, her skirt moulded to her body. I looked away and picked my way down until the sand softened my step. She never asked for my hand and I never offered. I made for a flat rock back against the shadows. She followed slowly. I sat down and patted a place next to me. She sat down on the edge of the rock, on the edge of my life.

Chapter Twenty Seven

I started to talk. Told her about all the colours that touched me. Purple for the hills. The evening emerald on the river. Blue silence. Images of the end, of dusk, of dreams, of death. Of the platonic Republic to which so many gave their lives in love. Some to find exile in the province of London. A state of everlasting loneliness. Of the dark and endless winter night. Of being eight and alone, and afraid. I fell quiet. She got up without a word and walked off, down to the shore. I watched her move, swaying a little on the uneven sand. It wasn't enough. She wanted the power of the priest. The kneeling in the dark. The peering thro' the grille. The crawling back into my past life. Behind the curtain I'd drawn so flimsy over my life. To be able to say "ego te absolvo" and drop her shoulders for my emphatic defeat.

Her head turned towards the bridge. She was standing very still as if listening for some faint sound. Time was passing but I wasn't conscious of the measure. It must be close to another day. The dance would be over. The fire only a smoulder. Patches would be curled up in bed. My father would have set the alarm for seven. The house would be in darkness. Only my mother would leave the hall light on for me.

I stood up, a little stiff from the cold rock. It was dark. The hour before dawn? I watched her from the rock. I found myself peering. Her white blouse was brimming with every breath she took. I went close. She half turned. I moved quickly up behind her. Pressed against her, my hand going round her waist, low on her stomach. My other hand turned her slight shoulder round. She was silent to my touch. Her lips were closed in a pout. I put my mouth low under her lips lifting them open. Soft and cold and lacking life. She started to say "tell me, tell me," when her lips were free. I closed them again in answer. Her lips clung for a second, them clamped shut and I took my mouth away and buried it in her neck. Her voice was insistent in my ear. "Tell me about my brother, tell me, tell me."

"No!"

Her voice changed, hardened as my hand left her waist to feel her breast through her blouse. Her body tensed to my touch. "No, tell me first." First? I stopped and made her look at me. Was she offering her body for my confession? Had her sense of sin succumbed to my silence? She gave the answer in her face and bringing her lips to mine she pushed her tongue between my teeth for confirmation.

My last act of contrition. Filling in the details of that winter day. Coldly: skimming pebbles, rolling clouds. Daylight wintering. Two boys trying to be brave. The old house: haunted how are you! Cold concept at eight. Frightened by the unquiet grave of another eight year old. Landlords and evictions. Our ever-present past. Trees swaying like the gallows of old. Fingers of fear clutching at our throats. Scaring each other for strength. A game without any winner. The black chasm. Imitating the old lady. The earth still fresh on her grave. The supernatural life of her soul beginning, ascending in a dark dawn. December descending. Rain threatening. Tears flowing into the black wind. Calling my name over and over. A laugh rose out of the hole. Echoed eerily and faded in full. My shaky laugh from the hollow below the rim of the hole. The soft mossy saviour of my life. Breaking my fall so gently that I thought I was in bed. Awakening from a broken dream. Coldly.

I stopped again and she caressed me with her body, rubbing, enticing, warming. My hand under her blouse. Soft sounds over the sand escaped her. "Don't stop," she moaned and she meant talking as well as touching.

How I climbed out of the hollow. My heart wild. A surge of feeling exhaled my pent-up breath. Then I was running, no, racing after him. Reaching the road before him by ducking between the trees for cover. All in my mind was to surprise him. To make him jump out of his skin at the sight of me. Over the wall of stones without knocking any off. Breaking into a trot down the Lawn height. Intending to leap out at him from the graveyard road. Waiting against the ditch. Waiting as the cold wind made my face red-raw. Waiting no more. Peeping out once to see his slight figure huddled into himself. Walking unwillingly in the fierce cold. I couldn't delay any longer. Keeping close to the ditch I hurried to the bend in the road. I thought I'd wait for him in the shelter of the high trees beyond the bend. Trees that hung both sides like a heavy green canopy even in the wildest winter. Rounding the turn was like walking into a valley. The wet wind ceased. Only the tops of trees rustled. Some rain scattered when the trees couldn't contain a gust. I slowed down to a walk. I loitered, idly grabbing sally rods from the ditch. Still he didn't show. "Slowcoach," I thought and continued to stroll.

I paused, tugging her blouse at the back, out of her skirt. Inside the waist-band I warmed my hands on her soft bottom. She tensed and her body went hard in my hands. "Go on," she breathed. "Finish it once and for all." She relaxed against me, letting my hands caress her without caring. I prepared myself for the final say.

I continued to stroll ...... to walk...... How I found myself at the latter end of the bridge. With no hiding place to spring from, except...

"What," she uttered as I stumbled again.

"Give me half a chance." I was clinging to her for a lifeline. For pain and pity...... "Help me, please," a rare word at home. She held me away, unbuttoning her blouse with one hand. At last, at last, I had my hands seared by the heavy heat of her breasts. I couldn't fondle them fast enough for my shaking fingers.

"It was cold on the bridge," I told her and she said, "I know, I know," as I lowered my mouth to kiss her breasts. Her blouse was hanging from her arms where I'd pushed it back. A breeze blew over her naked body, causing it to shiver in my mouth. Her nipple hard and bitter like a sloe. My mouth passed from peak to peak to lie crushed against her cleft. Gently I lowered her to the soft summer sands. On my knees before her.

"Bless me Father for I have sinned it's six years since my last

Confession. I was disobedient, two times, I told a lie one time, I had impure thoughts ten times, I said bad words four times, I didn't say my morning prayers, I don't know how many times"

"Night prayers, my child?"

"Now and never."

"Anything else now, my child?"

"Go on," she whispered leaning back against my arms.

"Go on, my child"

"I have sinned grievously Father"

"Against what Commandment, my child?"

"The fifth, Father"

"Was there grave matter?"

"Yes, Father"

"Did you have perfect knowledge?"

"No, Father"

"Did the grave matter have your full consent?"

"No, Father"

"Well my child, you know the three conditions. There's no mortal stain on your soul."

"But go on my child, tell me about it"

"Please tell me." Her skirt was tempted to rise as she strained back.

"No hiding place......except the turnstile to the strand."

"Up there?" and she pointed and her breasts had prominence in my hands.

"Yes," I could answer questions. Say no, or nod.

I pushed my mind out into the cold. Waiting at the bridge. Looking down into the water. So intently that the bridge moved. Dizzy with delight I waited for him. To show him I could travel across water on a concrete bridge. I was transported into another time, without...... dawn or dusk. A stillborn world. Of waiting and wending in the same spell. When he came upon me the water was still flowing away with my eyes. My legs only were seaworthy. My head was spinning on my shoulders. Hearing his first halting step on the bridge. Ducking down and gaining the top step. I called out his name.

She said his name softly to herself. I ceased talking.

My hands were around her waist and I unclasped them,

letting her rest back on her heels. Her skirt was riding high on her thighs. The white ring was visible where the sun hadn't strayed. Her legs were slightly parted for balance. I put a hand on the dark brown sheen above her knees. Up and up as she repeated his name. Higher and higher as his name changed to mine on her lips. She stopped my hand on the bare border.

I called out his name......and as if my voice cut the raw night to the quick, he cried out. I felt my way with my feet to the second step. He appeared on the ledge a tiny transfiguration against the night. I put out my hand. "Look!" I screeched, "touch me, I'm a ghost," and I cackled like an old woman. "I thought," he began......and he never finished his sentence. He tried to touch my hand as he spoke. Next I knew he was tumbling out over my head slapping my shoulder with a wet wellington.

The tide was in, a full tide, heavy with the rains. He couldn't swim a stroke. I was purchased to the steps with panic. Nothing moved in my body. Only my eyes. Only my eyes keeping vigil over his grave in the deep. Two times I saw him surface to cling to the rim of a whirlpool. The third time he didn't rise. "On the third day He arose again from the dead."

She took her hands away from where they had stayed my fondling. Whispering something......a prayer......or a poem.

> "Silent, O Moyle, be the roar of thy water,
> Break not, ye breezes, your chain of repose,
> While murmuring mournfully Lir's lonely daughter,
> Tells to the night star her tale of woes."

"I'm eternally sorry," I said. My body was still tense. My head was light. She was lying flat against the sand. Her blouse was still open to the waist. As she lay back her stomach flattened. Her skirt was rumpled up around her hips. She spoke again, eyes closed to the sky. "Sorrow is for life, not for all time." She put her hand out to me, unsmilingly, eyes half open. My hand missed her healing hand, finding her thighs. She moved slightly to let my hands rise. Inside and outside the soft silk. Getting warm and warmer as I touched the rim of elastic. For the first time she broke the silence, moaning and widening

180

her legs as if my hands were too much for her. She called out my name, his name. Together. I fell on top of her, my hands lifting her bottom. I pressed my mouth under her raised skirt to taste her thighs. She caught her breath and released some hard words. Poetry of pain. Sensual softness to lessen the blame. "You finished him, you finished him off."

"Finish me, finish me off." Her voice had changed, aged and fallowed. I was mesmerised by her clutching hands as they tore my shirt from my back. Her eyes flashing and wild and wanton as she arched under me. Her head moved from side to side in time to her frenzied feelings. Then it was all. Her mouth, her breasts, her thighs drove my mouth and hands to release my body. I came to my senses as her breasts faded to a white vapour.

Inert. The river lapped about our bodies. The sky was solemn overhead. No sound of man or beast broke into our breathlessness. A stain appeared on her thigh. Tears started slowly in her eyes. A muffled keen for the dead. For innocences. I fell away from her, the sand sucking wetly at my body. I waited by her side. She dried her own tears on her blouse. Buttoned up her body from the cold. A word. I waited for a word. Let it be Latin, I hoped. The sacred sound of forgiveness. "Ego te absolvo."

"What use am I now! I have sinned with you. I'm bleeding by your bloodstained hands." She spoke without looking at me. Bitter. Like the Old Woman of the Road. I was on my feet instantly, buttoning up my shirt. Tears stinging my cheeks. Running blind for the bridge. No answer,. No words on my lips. Nothing to say or gain.

My last act of contrition. The summer exploding. Black ashes on the earth. My secret soul broken over her innocent body. "This is my Blood." The Republic redeemed. The rest is silence.

I returned empty to an empty field. An empty skyline traced dawn across an empty sky. Silence. Only my screamed name challenged. Named for life...... "Michael! Michael! Michael! My name and silence. Perpetual.

A Strange Kind of Loving

by Sheila Mooney

A touching, searingly honest and at times heartbreaking account of an upbringing in an Ascendancy family and the author's vain attempts to win the love and approval of her Victorian father while continuing to support her beautiful, eccentric and alcoholic mother. Sheila Mooney is the sister of 1930s Hollywood idol, Maureen O'Sullivan, and her memoir contains witty and illuminating accounts of her career.

POOLBEG

Strange Vagabond of God
The Story of John Bradburne

Fr John Dove SJ

A re-issue of this popular and significant book

This is the story of the life of a remarkable religious service, in Europe, the Holy Land and Africa. Poet, mystic, hermit and vagabond, John Bradburne's strange life was devoted to the welfare of others and also a ceaseless quest for God. Since his death, there have been moves towards a campaign for his beatification.

POOLBEG

The Poolbeg Golden Treasury of Well Loved Poems

Edited by Sean McMahon

By the compiler of *Rich and Rare*
and
The Poolbeg Book of Children's Verse

A delightful anthology of everyone's favourite poems, from Shakespeare to Patrick Kavanagh

POOLBEG